Who Killed Doctor

Silver Cartwheel?

By Gary Christenson

November 2015

Also by Gary Christenson

Non-Fiction:

"Gold Value and Gold Prices From 1971 – 2021 - An Empirical Model"

Who Killed Doctor Silver Cartwheel?

The views expressed in this work are solely those of the author. This is a work of fiction. Names, characters, places, and incidents either are the product of the author's imagination or are used fictionally. Any resemblance to actual persons, living or dead, businesses, companies, events or locals is coincidental.

The author of this book does not dispense financial advice. The author's intent is solely to offer entertainment and general information to assist others in their quest for financial understanding and success.

ISBN: 9781518739576

For Diana

Contents

INTRODUCTION

Silver coins were widely used for daily transactions in the first half of the 20th century in the United States as well as many other countries. They have since disappeared, prices for consumer goods and services are much higher, and nearly everyone understands that much is wrong with our financial systems.

What went wrong?

Detective Zach Chandler investigates why silver was demonetized and is no longer used in coins in the United States.

He also examines fiat currency, central banking, the story of silver, and he makes his best estimate for silver prices in the year 2020.

Chapter 1

I looked at the picture of Philip Marlowe on the wall and whispered, "What would you do?"

He looked back and gruffly suggested, "Figure it out yourself."

Humphrey Bogart as Sam Spade stared at me from the adjacent wall. He was no help either.

Silver paperweights sitting on my desk would have been more helpful than the legendary detectives staring at me from my office walls.

I went back to my report for Mrs. Garibaldi. She was an attractive 45-year-old second wife of a Councilman here in Dallas, Texas, and probably about to be divorced, based on the pictures I intended to show her. She hired me a month ago to follow her husband, take pictures, and confirm that he was having an affair.

My name is Zach Chandler and I'm a private detective. I don't do Google, I don't own a computer, I have no cell phone, and some say I'm a throwback to the 1950s. I carry a six shot 38 revolver and have no interest in a 9mm handgun with 16 in the clip. I talk to people, think about what they tell me, about what they're not telling me, and why they're lying. I'm good at my job and I make a decent living but I'll never be rich.

In my youth I was a bit taller than 6'2", muscular and good looking. Now I'm a Vietnam vet, older, grey, a widower, much wiser, and getting by. I like old movies, chess, murder mysteries, baseball, and intelligent people.

I do divorce work when I have nothing else that pays. This job was divorce work, following a hound dog councilman who was bed-hopping in not one, but two affairs, while lying to a neglected wife at home. It was easy work, he didn't expect to be followed, and even though he was clever, he wasn't devious enough to hide from me.

I had watched him leave council chambers and followed him to a downtown hotel. It was the usual game, rent a hotel room, wait for your girlfriend, pay the bill in cash, and create no credit card record. I had a good idea of what would happen in the hotel bed. His girlfriend was a gorgeous vice president at one of the largest banks in Dallas, the City Bank of Texas. She was 15 years younger than his current wife, well-dressed, athletic, and hustling business through extra-special activities with the councilman.

I heard the bell that announced someone had entered the outer office. Hilda would greet and manage her, inform me she was waiting, and give me a signal. Hilda had seen it all and usually had people figured in about a minute. It takes me longer so I listen to Hilda.

"Mrs. Garibaldi is here to see you." Hilda announced it with just a hint of deference. She didn't like Mrs. Garibaldi because Mrs. Garibaldi thought she was special. Hilda is irritated by self-absorbed people who think the world revolves around them.

"Mrs. Garibaldi, thank you for coming to my office." I tried for neutral, friendly but businesslike. I had bad news for her and didn't want to be chummy.

She entered and frowned involuntarily. She was slumming, but I ignored it. I pointed to a comfortable chair in front of my unimpressive desk and invited her to sit. She sat, crossed her legs, settled in, and starred at me for at least ten seconds. I figured she was preparing for an unpleasant situation.

"Mr. Chandler, I'm here for the bad news, or the surprise that there is no bad news. I have another appointment so let's get right to it." She had stunning blue eyes, high cheekbones, and a sultry and sexy presence that would have brought her almost anything she wanted when she was 25. At 45 she looked great, but I assumed her husband thought of her as last year's model and wanted to trade up. It was his loss.

"Well, Mrs. Garibaldi, I truly wish I could surprise you, but as you suggested, there is bad news. Your husband leads an active social life, hides it moderately well, and led me on several interesting chases. The bottom line is that I observed him on five occasions meeting a woman named Clarisse at several hotels, and once at an apartment. I also have pictures of him chatting with another woman in a lounge, pictures of him entering her home a few hours later, and leaving her home well after midnight."

I let the bad news settle into the room, watched her eyes, and saw her shoulders slump slightly. She was a proud woman who knew the truth in her heart, had been hoping to hear otherwise, and now had to face it. It took her a few moments before she could tell me, "I trust everything you told me, but I need to see pictures."

I took a stack of pictures, all 8x10's, and handed them to her. The first four were pictures of her husband and Clarisse obviously enjoying a conversation. The next five pictures had been taken with a long lens in less than ideal conditions from a good location. They had been so anxious for each other they neglected to close the blinds. I had made the extra effort to place myself and my camera in a higher room where I could see through their open blinds. Those five pictures left nothing to the imagination as to what they were doing. I saw Mrs. Garibaldi's face tighten and heard her sigh. It was an ugly business and about to get worse.

She looked at me with sad but determined eyes and said, "I expected this but it's still a shock."

I waited while she pulled herself together. She told me, "You know my husband is a councilman, a very important councilman in his opinion. He has political ambitions, hopes to be the next governor of Texas, and dreams of being President someday. There is enough scandal in his life already and I don't want to make it worse, but I do need the truth."

She had more to say. I waited.

"I came to you because you were highly recommended as competent and more importantly as discrete. One of my friends praised you extensively. I don't want to destroy my husband's grandiose political ambitions, even though he is a lying cheating snake. So I'm asking that you keep this quiet and make certain your files, notes, and pictures never see the light of day. He wants to be President and I'd like to be first lady, and that won't happen if this affair is widely publicized."

I looked at her with new appreciation and told her, "I'll destroy most of the notes and pictures and these will be digitized and encrypted and only Hilda, my secretary, will have access. I don't use a computer so I can't disclose anything."

She sighed again and asked how much she owed me. I told her I would send her a bill, itemized as much as she wanted, but my guess was around $7,000. She said she would rather write a check today.

She went back to studying the pictures and I saw a devilish smile slowly crawl across her face. She asked rhetorically if I thought the councilman was screwing the banker or vice versa.

I didn't reply and waited while she made her decisions. Finally she said, "I'm going to take these pictures. I'll call back in a week if I want anything else, and you can tell me if I owe any balance beyond this check." She handed me a check and I barely glanced at it.

"That will be fine, Mrs. Garibaldi. I'll have a final tally for you in a few days, and I'll provide anything else you want."

She smiled, and although it looked strained, I could see the flash of beauty and decency within her. I liked her and assumed I would never see her again. She stood, stuck out her hand, and left with her pictures, worries, and ambitions.

After she left I told Hilda the arrangements we had made and I settled into my chair to read the morning paper. It appeared that the bankers and politicians were in bed with each other in Dallas, Washington, New York, Tokyo, London, and every other major city. It was business as usual and for the most part I accepted politics as nothing more than annoying mosquitos sucking blood.

I read the obituaries, checked local news, looked for potential business, and thought I would mosey down to the local coffee shop for a cup while I decided what to do next.

I was about to leave when the bell rang in the outer office. It could have been anyone but on the chance it was new business I sat down and waited. Two minutes later Hilda walked in, closed the door behind her, and said, "A Mrs. Mildred MacDougall is here to see you." She whispered, "Watch out boss, she's way smarter than she lets on." She smiled sweetly, saw my nod, opened the office door and invited Mrs. MacDougall into my office.

I stood and observed a well preserved lady who looked about 75. She walked slowly into my office appearing fragile, unsteady on her feet, and a bit uncertain. That initial assessment evaporated the moment she spoke.

"Mr. Chandler, I am Mildred MacDougall, and I've heard good things about you. May I sit down?"

Her voice was firm and strong and I took her for a natural leader. Her eyes were intense, cold, and gray. She looked at me and I felt like I was a short magazine article she had read in a heartbeat. I waved at the chair where she should sit, but she was already settling in, making herself comfortable, and I felt like her presence filled the office. It was an unusual feeling.

"Mr. Chandler, I'd like you to do something for me."

There was no question about whether or not I wanted the job. She had just assumed that I was working for her the moment she walked into my office. I knew this would be interesting.

"Mrs. MacDougall, how can I help you?"

"Mr. Chandler, I know your time is valuable, but I'm going to digress for a moment to give you some background information. My father had a collection of silver dollars which he loved. He called them cartwheels, which I understand was a typical nickname for silver dollars. I remember him taking me to the drugstore, back in ancient times, to eat ice cream cones as we sat on stools at the counter. You may not be old enough to remember, but drugstores had soda counters and sold ice cream and were friendly to people decades ago when I was a little girl. The important point is that he paid for our ice cream cones with a silver dollar, and got change back in silver coins."

She focused those intense gray eyes upon me and I believed that her father and those silver dollars were the most important things in the world.

"Mr. Chandler, I want to know what happened to those silver dollars. Now I carry this nasty folding paper stuff or worse, plastic cards. There is no joy in the money these days, it is dishonest, and it doesn't even feel like money. It is nothing but pretend paper that buys less every day. Worse, I think most people don't realize how degraded it has become. So Mr. Chandler, my questions are what happened to those silver dollars, and why aren't they still used as money?"

I didn't know what to say. People come to me because I'm a detective and I find missing persons, follow people, spy on spouses and business partners, solve murders, and sometimes I accompany clients as an expensive bodyguard. But I've never been asked to investigate why silver dollars are no longer circulated as money. I had no ideas, but I was certain this lady would know where to start, and that she fully expected me to give her a comprehensive, intelligent, and complete answer. Strange indeed!

"Now I understand you are a detective. I want you to do your detective thing and find out why this happened. Why do we have funny money, inflation, pieces of paper that purchase so little, central banks doing dishonest things with our money, and so on? I want to know what happened to silver dollars before I die." She looked at me like this was the most logical request in the world.

"Mrs. MacDougall, there must be many ways to locate the information you want. I'll bet there are hundreds of books at the Barnes & Noble down the street that explain what happened. Probably there are thousands of stories on the Internet that will explain more than you ever want to know about what happened to our money, and why those silver dollars that your father loved are no longer in circulation. Mrs. MacDougall I don't think I'm the right person for this job."

"Mr. Chandler, I've learned a thing or two in my 85 years and I think you are the man for the job. I want the personal touch, I'm not interested in Google searches, and I don't want to read books written by economists or politicians. They are mostly liars and thieves and I wouldn't believe what they say anyway."

So she was 85 years old, not 75, and her mental acuity and presence would leave most people in the dust. She didn't like politicians and I liked her more with each passing minute. But I was still the wrong person for the job because I knew nothing about economics, modern finance, silver dollars, or money. All I knew was that our money buys less each day and I needed more of it.

I shook my head and started to tell her again that I was the wrong person for the job, but I never got started.

"No, I want you to find out and report back to me. And don't bring me any self-serving nonsense from Nobel Prize winners or Federal Reserve people either. I want straight, simple facts and reasonable interpretations that pass the common sense test. Just because people are intelligent, use fancy words, and are skilled with mathematical gobbledygook does not mean they know the first thing about silver, genuine money or real economics."

I made one more effort to dissuade her, but she wouldn't budge. She wanted me. I liked the feeling and wondered about the rest of the story.

"Mr. Chandler, you investigate murders, right? Well I want this murder investigated! Who killed the silver dollar and those beautiful silver coins that we used for daily commerce when I was a child? My dad used to call it Doctor Silver because he said silver was a natural healer for economic and physical diseases, and silver dollars were cartwheels, so he called them Doctor Silver Cartwheels. I want to know who killed Doctor Silver Cartwheel!"

She paused, looked at me with a twinkle in her eyes, and said, "Pardon my digression, but I really do want you to investigate the death of Doctor Silver Cartwheel."

It took me a moment, but eventually I told her I would work for her, named a price plus expenses, and we chatted more about what she wanted. She reminisced about her childhood, what she had seen decades ago, things her father had told her about silver dollars, gold coins, honest money, and days gone by. By the time she left I was completely charmed. She could have been my favorite aunt.

Chapter 2

I'm a detective investigating a murder. Murders are unique and individual but there are patterns. What motivates the murder? Is it money, sex, jealousy, greed, power, or anger? I've seen them all. What means did they use to kill? Was it a gun, a knife, a club, or poison? What opportunity did the murderer have to kill the victim?

But the basic questions in a murder investigation are simple. Was there a crime? Where is the body? If there was no body and no crime I was wasting my time and her money.

How do I find a body in the murder investigation of Doctor Silver Cartwheel? I knew where to look.

"Hilda, I'm driving to the library. Hold down the fort."
She looked at me like she had 1,000 times before. She might as
well have said, "I don't understand, you'll probably tell me
when you want to, and I don't really care anyway." She
waved and looked back to whatever was on her computer,
probably recipes that fit her weird eating habits, which
partially explained why she was healthier than me. I walked
down to my car thinking about Mrs. MacDougall.

I drive a white three year old Camry that blends with
Dallas traffic so it is difficult to spot when I'm tailing
someone. I turned right out of the lot and drove to the Dallas
Public Library. Every other detective would have fired up
their computer and Googled it. I liked my way better.

I spoke to my favorite librarian, teased her a little about
nothing special, and sat down to read and take notes after she
brought me a stack of books. It had taken me less than three
minutes to explain my interest and she knew exactly where to
start.

I learned that in 1964 one of our most corrupt
presidents, Lyndon B. Johnson, from the great state of Texas
that I call home, had demonetized silver. I read more and
filled in a few blanks. Dollars, half dollars, quarters, and
dimes had been 90% silver until Johnson removed the silver
and substituted copper. I remembered that real silver coins
had a ring to them but I hadn't heard it in 40 or 50 years.
Johnson had killed silver coins because silver had become too
expensive. Another book told me that it wasn't silver
becoming expensive, but dollars buying less, which made
more sense. My last cup of coffee at that diner sold for $2.25
with one refill. I remembered a cup of coffee in the 1960s
selling for a dime with free refills. Our money bought less.

I believed the story that dollars were worth less, not yet worthless, but worth less, and that was why silver was more expensive when priced in dollars. The same thing happened with gold.

Why?

I skipped the yak-yak from the politicians and read more about Johnson breaking the bank with huge spending on the Vietnam War and his phony War on Poverty. It was par for the course with politicians. Spend money, buy votes, screw the taxpayers, run up the debt, create inflation, and blame somebody else. Bottom line, the government spent too much money, put that money into circulation, and prices went up. I wondered how much the price of a cup of coffee had increased between 1960 and 1970.

It all made sense when I remembered the Vietnam craziness, being drafted, slogging through rice paddies, and wondering why we were fighting. Later I found out that the war was mostly about money, oil, politics, and expanding the military. I hadn't forgotten but I had made my peace with it. My last Vietnam nightmare had been years ago.

Next I read about Gresham's Law. The example given was perfect for my investigation. Silver dollars were more valuable than the fakes made from copper. People realized, regardless of what the politicians claimed, that silver dollars had real value. They were 90% silver and silver had been valuable since before the Christian era. It reminded me that Jesus had been betrayed for 30 pieces of silver, not 30 slips of colored paper. People hoarded the real silver dollars, half dollars, quarters and dimes, and let the new copper fakes circulate.

I removed the 3 quarters I had in my pants pocket and looked at them. Yup, it was easy to see. They had a shiny veneer that covered a copper center. I dropped one to hear the metallic ring and instead heard a dull clunking sound. Two people looked up from their reading and wondered why I had dropped a coin. I smiled at them, leaned down to retrieve my quarter, and continued my education.

The United States government during the Vietnam era had increased their debt by $125 Billion, which was a lot of money back then. I checked the average hourly wage for 1970 and discovered it was about $3.50. I divided and found that the debt had increased by the equivalent of 35 billion man hours. Impressive, but so what?

Then a nasty thought occurred to me. What if silver dollars actually weren't common? What if Mrs. MacDougall and I remembered an exaggeration? I asked the librarian for more information on minting silver dollars. The reference books informed me that a huge number of silver dollars had been minted – something like 500 million between 1880 and 1921.

I found another book on Las Vegas history and looked for pictures of slot machines from the 1950's. Las Vegas had thousands of slot machines that took coins, from pennies to silver dollars. If Las Vegas catered to silver dollars, they had been real and common in the 1950s. Doctor Silver Cartwheel had been alive and well in the 1950's.

I read for another hour and realized I was missing something, but I didn't know what. Maybe I should visit a United States Mint and read their history, or maybe I would scan newspapers from the early 1960's to better understand the economy at the time. I looked at my watch and decided to drive home and forget about the Vietnam War, bankers, politicians, and silver dollars.

Chapter 3

I woke the next morning knowing I needed professional help. I drove to the office and said hi to Hilda as she checked me for signs of a hangover. She disapproved of drinking more than one per night, and knew that in my younger years I had used a sliding limit between 7 and 10. I had occasional hangovers in years past and had forced myself to suffer through both her critical assessments and the hangovers.

"Morning boss. No calls yet. How are you doing on Mrs. MacDougall's request?"

"I need help. I need to learn more about silver dollars. Can you find two or three coin stores close by? I want a big one so I can chat up the manager."

"Sure boss, I'll find several, make a few calls, and pick the best two."

I had no doubt she would do exactly that. She has a sense for people lying to her and she cuts through their stupidity and nonsense quickly. I went into my office, grabbed the morning paper, and looked for news stories about rare coins, inflation, Vietnam, and anything related to silver. What I found was practically nothing. Vietnam was ancient history and our good friend these days, silver was mentioned nowhere except in a story about a "Silver Anniversary," and according to the newspapers, inflation was missing in action. My food and insurance bill suggested otherwise, but who argues with official statistics?

An hour later Hilda knocked on my door, entered, and handed me a piece of paper. She smiled and said, "You'll like the top one," and walked out.

The first name was Mystic Coins on Oak Lawn Blvd. in Dallas, less than half an hour away. I liked the name and I trusted Hilda. I decided to start there, so I left my office, told Hilda I'd be back later, and made the short drive to Mystic Coins.

It turned out that Mystic Coins was on the 9th floor of a large office building that housed insurance agents, accountants, a boutique brokerage operation, a credit counseling service, and of course, many attorneys. I took the elevator to the 9th floor, turned left and was pleasantly surprised to see that Mystic Coins occupied nearly half of the floor. I added a zero to my previous estimate of their annual revenue and entered their office.

The lady at the reception desk seemed intelligent, verbal, and intense. I tried to explain what I wanted and within a minute she was telling me what I needed far better than I knew. I shut up and listened while she explained the services they offered, why those services were valuable, and told me I should chat with Mr. Mystic, the owner. She pressed a button, spoke into the intercom for a moment, and buzzed me through the door. I looked around the retail sales floor, saw a number of display cases containing shiny gold and silver things, five employees talking with clients, and several more office doors toward the back. A moment later a man emerged from his office and walked toward me.

"Mr. Mystic, I presume."

"Yes, I'm Grant Mystic, and you are Mr. Chandler?" He offered his hand, gave me a firm handshake and said, "Welcome to my world. I think you'll find it interesting and unusual. Come back to my office and tell me what you have on your mind."

He turned and beckoned for me to follow. He reminded me of Mrs. MacDougall, immediately in charge, friendly, and intelligent. I followed him, observing his business as I walked, and thought his operation was impressive.

He directed me to one of several leather chairs around a small table, asked if I wanted coffee, and when I declined, he sat, folded his hands in his lap, and said, "Mr. Chandler, what can I do for you?"

He gazed at me with an expression that suggested he had seen everything and nothing I said would surprise him. He seemed perfectly relaxed, focused upon me, intensely present, and more than a little strange. I saw no halo but he was the kind of guy who might have light radiating from his head. I hesitated and he smiled. He knew the effect he had upon people.

"Mr. Mystic, I'm a private detective on a case, perhaps the strangest in my experience, and I need perspective. I went to the library yesterday and absorbed background information but today I'm here to ask you about silver dollars and why they are no longer in circulation."

He absorbed the information as if I had asked about purchasing a crescent wrench. A moment later he flashed a warm smile and said, "Strangely enough, I discussed that topic a few weeks ago with one of my better customers. You might know her, about 85 years old with a sharp mind and strong opinions."

My face must have betrayed me. I seldom let that happen.

"So I see that you know Mrs. MacDougall. We have some common ground. Well, I'm at your service. What can I do to help?"

I found it impossible not to like him. He was charming without phoniness, intelligent but not arrogant, and he seemed wise. Hilda would say he was an old soul, whatever that means. I just wanted information and understanding and he probably had both.

"My client has a nostalgic interest in silver and silver dollars, and wants me, a detective, not an economist or historian, to explain why silver dollars are no longer in circulation. I remember silver dollars, but they disappeared in my teens, so I don't have the emotional connection that my client has, since she is considerably older than I am. Mr. Mystic, I hope you will explain what happened and why silver was demonetized."

He started slowly, feeling his way around my unfamiliarity with the topic. "The United States was founded on the idea of honest money. By that I mean money that can't be created by a politician or banker. If gold and silver are money, the amount of money increases only as more gold and silver are mined, or as we exchange trade goods for gold and silver. Money supply increases slowly, prices are relatively stable, perhaps they slowly decrease, and the focus is on manufacturing and production, not monetary engineering and the creation of paper assets."

He paused to see if I understood. Apparently he was satisfied that he had not lost me, so he continued. "I'm not saying the system was perfect or ideal, but it worked with some reservations. Of course, human emotions are always relevant, and those who worship at the altars of greed and power inevitably want to change the system to benefit themselves. Their sales pitch was that they could stabilize the economic system by implementing a central bank, owned by other banks, and the bankers would manage the creation and printing of the money. You can see how poorly that worked, but we don't need to explore that rat-hole today."

I think he was worried that I was blind regarding the government and that I believed banker propaganda. I reassured him and directed him back on the track I wanted. "I paid $2.25 for a cup of coffee yesterday, and I remember paying a dime for a cup of coffee back in the 60's. I doubt our economic system is better for the average Joe, and it certainly has not created stable prices. But I have no doubt that the current system works well for bankers and politicians and paper pushers. But you were saying about silver…" I let the sentence trail off, hoping he would get back to silver.

He smiled at me. I think behind his charm and wisdom was a touch of sadness. Instead of telling me about silver, he motioned for me to follow him. "I want to show you something that will help you understand. Like most people, you know something is wrong, but you don't understand what or why. They say fish aren't aware of water, and we are like fish living our whole lives inside the financial system. It is difficult to conceive of a different system."

He held the door for me and said, "We are going to that window." He pointed to a wall of windows that looked south.

We walked to the window and I admired the view. I could see the Dallas skyline, which was pretty at night and passable during the day, but he wasn't interested in the skyline.

"Look over there." He pointed in the general direction of downtown. "It looks like a modern and thriving city, but a closer look shows many homeless people, runaways living on the streets, drug-dealers, panhandlers, modern soup kitchens, homeless shelters, and various government offices promoting welfare, food stamps, and a dozen other benefit programs. I haven't even mentioned organized crime, insurance fraud, massive white-collar fraud, and who knows what happens behind closed doors in the banking world."

I had seen most of what he had mentioned while working the streets. The bankers and politicians were secretive and I vaguely understood what they did but mostly I wasn't interested. What Mr. Mystic had told me was no shock.

"You see what I'm talking about?

"I have worked the streets and I know about the human condition on the margin, but what does that have to do with silver and money?"

He looked at me, disappointed I think, and said, "We have debased the money by creating far too much of it. When money is devalued the purchasing power of the currency, public morality, and the spirit of the country are gradually destroyed. It has happened before and it will happen again. Neither you nor I will change it, but I want to show you an alternative."

He pointed in another direction and I figured he would give me a sales pitch on buying silver and gold since it was his business.

Instead he took me to a door marked "Private" and opened it with a key and a digital code. He gave me a stern expression and said, "This room is seldom used. I hope you appreciate what I am about to show you." He walked into the unlit room, flipped on some lights and waited for me to enter. He closed the door and walked toward a window.

I felt a tingle on the back of my neck, and strange warmth spread through my gut. I felt relaxed and confident. I pushed the relaxed feeling aside and became intensely alert. Mr. Mystic waited for me in front of a long window that ran almost the length of the room. I joined him and looked at the city.

"Look out this window and observe Dallas from a different perspective."

What I saw looked about the same, but there were differences. The skyline seemed less developed and somehow Dallas looked more beautiful and hospitable from this direction. The traffic was lighter and I saw more people walking and riding bicycles. I saw several parks I didn't remember. I knew I was looking at Dallas, but it almost seemed like a different city. It was strange in more ways than I had initially observed.

"What you see is a bit more pleasant than you expected, don't you think?"

He didn't wait for me to answer. He must have seen the puzzled expression on my face. "But what you don't see is the most important part. For instance, you don't see as many banks, you see very few people living on the streets, fewer homeless shelters since they aren't needed, and there are fewer cops patrolling the streets. There is more employment, a smaller drug problem, and generally speaking people are happier, healthier, and enjoy a better standard of living. This world has all the same problems, joys, and diversions that you saw in the other one, but it is a better world."

I must have looked confused. It was Dallas, right? How could it be a different world?

Mystic smiled with no humor implied, and said, "That's right. This is Dallas in a world that could have been. In this world the Federal Reserve is far smaller and less important, President Kennedy was not assassinated, and dollars are partially backed by gold. A cup of coffee costs about twenty-five cents, bank operations have changed little since the 1950s, the military is much smaller, the United States is still a beacon for freedom loving emigrants, and, in my opinion, it is a far more pleasant world. By the way, the USSR collapsed in this world, and politicians are still liars."

I must have looked stunned. I felt like my head was spinning. I was stuck on the different world idea and I couldn't see how this could be a different world. Mr. Mystic let me think while I steadied myself by touching the wall. I looked more carefully at the city and saw that it really was different. There were buildings that I had not seen before, parks that had not existed yesterday, and cars that looked like cars, but the models were unfamiliar. I knew for certain that most people did not walk or ride bicycles in Dallas, unlike what I saw before me.

Mr. Mystic gave me an understanding smile. He said, "You see, in the world in which you and I live, we made choices that placed the military and the bankers in charge. Of course we pretend that the politicians run the country, but that is mostly misdirection and nonsense. The bankers and the military owned the politicians so the country changed to benefit the bankers, military and politicians. This world is basically the same, but the balance is different. The money in this alternate world is more honest, it is still loosely backed by gold, politicians pretend to follow a budget, there is little inflation, and very little debt. Consequently the financial and banking industry is a tiny fraction of what you and I consider normal, and the world runs better and more efficiently. Human nature hasn't changed so this world has its share of graft, corruption, greed, and useless wars, but on average, it has far less of those destructive forces. In my opinion this world is better for the average citizen, much better for the poor, and actually more pleasant for the political and financial elite, even if they are only rich, instead of obscenely wealthy."

He looked at me, saw my confusion, and said, "Take your time. It will make sense in a while. Only a few people have been inside this room, but I'm sure Mrs. MacDougall would approve."

I thought about what he had said, but it was difficult to visualize a cup of coffee costing only a quarter, money backed by gold, banks that weren't exceedingly powerful, and ... I lost my train of thought and just stared down at the streets. Maybe it was a better world, and maybe Mr. Mystic was a hypnotist and I was actually sitting in his office dreaming while he implanted hypnotic suggestions. Maybe I was losing my mind thinking about alternate worlds. My hands started to shake and I felt faint.

He took my arm, steadied me, and quietly suggested, "I think it is time to return to your regular world."

We walked out of that strange room and I appreciated his support. I didn't think I would faint, but my legs were weak and my balance was off. He gently pushed me out the door and locked it. Mr. Mystic slowly assisted me back to his office and told me to sit.

He must have left his office but I was too dazed to remember. I remember him handing me a cup of black coffee and hearing, "Drink this. You'll be okay in half an hour."

I drank the coffee feeling like I had survived a car wreck. Gradually I came back and realized I was in his office and he was waiting patiently for me to return to normal consciousness.

"That room makes everyone who visits it feel faint. I had a rough time when I discovered it, so I understand how you feel. Can I get you another cup of coffee?"

"Yes, please." I remembered my manners but did not understand what had happened.

He left and returned with a half-full pot of coffee, poured me another cup and filled his own cup. He waited while I pulled myself together, slowly sipping hot coffee.

Finally I managed to say, "I don't understand what happened, but thank you for an interesting afternoon. I need some time to think."

"Come back anytime."

I got to my feet, felt more or less normal, and shook his hand. Ten minutes later I sat in my car thinking I truly needed a drink.

Instead of going to a bar I went to a 1950's diner where the waitresses dressed in poodle skirts and served great burgers and unbelievable fries. My waitress had been young when Kennedy had been killed and she looked out of place in a poodle skirt. We can't go backwards and we should move forward. Not everyone does.

I still liked my 1950's nostalgic world. I wolfed down the burger and fries, and followed them with a chocolate malt and apple pie. The poodle skirt swished down the aisle and dropped the check on my table. I verified it, like I always do, and saw that the burger was $9.95, the fries were $3.95, the malt was $3.45, and the pie was $4.95. With tax the meal was $24 and change. I remembered a 2nd date with cute young thing when I was 17. We had eaten burgers, fries and malts and the bill for both of us had been less than $3.00.

With my hunger satisfied I almost felt back to normal. Then I remembered Mr. Mystic saying that in alternate-Dallas a cup of coffee was $0.25. My $24.00 meal in alternate-Dallas probably would have cost less than three bucks.

What a load of crap! I didn't believe it and didn't want to believe it. It had to be hallucination or hypnosis. Suddenly I felt very tired. I left $27.00 on the table and drove home thinking about nothing.

Chapter 4

McDonald's Menu in the 1950s

I woke the next day, had two extra cups of coffee, and felt lousy. It wasn't the fries. Mr. Mystic crossed my mind a dozen times before I arrived at work. I thought alternate-Dallas was nonsense.

I grunted at Hilda and she smiled. I thought it was a superior and condescending smile but I might have overreacted. I shut my office door and read the newspaper. There were headlines about bailing out another bank and something about the FDIC being close to broke. An editorial ranted about bail-ins that could happen in the US, like the banks that stole from depositors in Cyprus in 2013. It made little sense to me.

I removed my wallet and picked out a $20 bill. I looked at it carefully for the first time. It said, "Federal Reserve Note," and Twenty Dollars and "This Note Is Legal Tender For All Debts, Public and Private." On the back I saw a picture of the White House and the words, "In God We Trust."

I pondered the $20 bill for a while and decided that my unofficial interpretation was that the politicians were in bed with the bankers, the White House had a mandate from God, we should trust God and politicians, and I still didn't know what "Federal Reserve Note" meant.

I hesitated and finally walked out to Hilda's desk and said, "I need you to research something." She looked at me like she always does, with a mixture of interest and skepticism. "I need to know what 'Federal Reserve Note' means." I showed her my $20 bill.

"I can tell you right now. There is no need to Google it. It means a note put into circulation by the Federal Reserve Bank that is a liability of the Federal Reserve Bank and an obligation of the US government. You don't have twenty dollars, you have a piece of paper that is a debt of the Federal Reserve. They owe you twenty dollars and this is their note or I.O.U. to you indicating such."

Hilda looked smug and I must have looked dumbfounded. She smiled and continued, "Worse, that note is a loan from the Federal Reserve that is backed by the assets of the Federal Reserve. Would you care to guess what those assets are?"

I know a loaded question when I hear it. "Just tell me."

"The assets that back the twenty bucks the Fed owes you are the bonds issued by the Treasury, you know, the $18+ Trillion in debt that the federal government officially owes and will never actually repay. So that twenty bucks is a debt to you from the Federal Reserve backed by the debt of the US government."

"So I'm a creditor of the banking system?"

Hilda was on a roll. "When I took Mrs. Garibaldi's check to the bank and deposited it, I put your money into the bank and now your money is safely stored at the bank." She paused for effect, showed a smirk on her face, and continued. "Nope, wrong answer! When I deposited that check into your account, you loaned the bank $7,000 and they acknowledged the debt by crediting your account. It is not your money, it is now the bank's money and they owe you. Oh, by the way, that will stand in court."

Hilda looked smug, like she had just popped my bubble and thought it was high time I woke up. I guess she saw the glazed expression on my face.

"So if your bank goes belly-up for whatever reason, you are a creditor of the bank and might get your money returned. The FDIC might come through for you, or maybe not. But don't worry, the government has your best interest at heart and they will take care of you."

Now she was being sarcastic. I countered with, "Banks fail all the time and nobody gets hurt if they have less than $100,000 or whatever in the bank."

Hilda tolerated my naiveté. She looked intently at me and said, "Probably correct, so far." Have I mentioned before that she is not a trusting soul when it comes to banks and politicians? Well, she isn't.

"So how do you know all this?" I did not doubt her. If she says it, you can take it to the bank, and then I realized how silly and ironic that sounded.

"My dad was a mathematician at UC Berkeley in the 60's, 70's, and 80's. I remember occasional rants about what Johnson did to the economy and what Nixon did to our money, and what the bankers had done to everyone, so I grew up with it. It was an unusual childhood."

"So my money in my checking account is actually a loan from me to the bank, the cash in my wallet is a debt from the Federal Reserve, and those loans are backed by nothing but loans and more debt. It sounds like the bankers and politicians have had their way with the American people."

"Yes, but don't worry about it. They have been working the same scam for decades. As long as banks trust each other and people trust the digital and paper dollars in circulation, it works. In a word, the entire system is based on confidence."

I was starting to understand. "And in 2008 when things almost collapsed, there was a confidence crisis and banks, major financial companies, and people were questioning if they would get paid. They lost confidence and the system practically collapsed."

"Yup. And the Fed created over $16 trillion to support the system and it worked, if you don't mind the ongoing recession, lots of unemployed workers, massive debts, and more wealth transfers to the already wealthy."

I was in over my head and I had heard enough. "Thanks for the explanation. I have a headache. I'm going out."

Hilda went back to whatever and I left.

Chapter 5

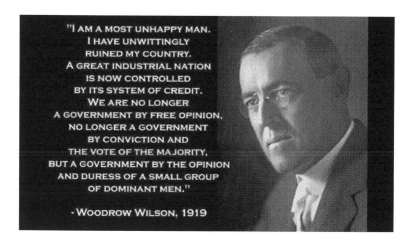

"I AM A MOST UNHAPPY MAN.
I HAVE UNWITTINGLY
RUINED MY COUNTRY.
A GREAT INDUSTRIAL NATION
IS NOW CONTROLLED
BY ITS SYSTEM OF CREDIT.
WE ARE NO LONGER
A GOVERNMENT BY FREE OPINION,
NO LONGER A GOVERNMENT
BY CONVICTION AND
THE VOTE OF THE MAJORITY,
BUT A GOVERNMENT BY THE OPINION
AND DURESS OF A SMALL GROUP
OF DOMINANT MEN."

- WOODROW WILSON, 1919

I felt dazed and disoriented. Between Hilda spouting off about dollars not being real money but a debt from the Fed, Mr. Mystic talking about alternate-Dallas, the bank taking my money and thanking me for the loan, and the comparison between the cost of the meal at the diner last night and when I was 17, I felt betrayed and bewildered. I remembered that movie, "The Matrix," and wondered if it was more insightful than I had realized.

Two cups of coffee later I had an idea. I had done some detective work a while back for a banker and we had gotten together every few months for a drink after hours. I found a payphone a block away, called him, left a message, and suggested we meet for a drink that afternoon at one of his favorite watering holes.

I went back to the office, thanked Hilda for the rant, and escaped into the security of my office. I decided to document on a yellow pad everything that had happened since Mrs. MacDougall had changed my life a few days ago. An hour later Fred Harper, my banker friend, called back and suggested we meet at one of his hangouts that afternoon at 4 pm. We agreed and I made more notes.

I handed my notes to Hilda on the way out, asked her to work her magic on them, and drove to meet Fred. He was semi-retired, astute, and had been in the banking world for decades. I liked him and forgave him his chosen profession.

He had arrived before me and was already sitting in a quiet booth. I guessed he was drinking Martinis. When the waitress arrived I ordered my usual beer and asked how he was doing.

"My golf handicap index is up to 12. I've been having back problems and I don't get full rotation, so my club head speed is down over 8 mph. My wife is taking three blood pressure meds, and my portfolio is up 27% since this time last year. I'm doing fine, considering. How about you?"

I told him my golf handicap was hovering around 18, I had no health issues other than 15 extra pounds, and business was so-so. We raised our drinks, toasted our local golfer, Jordan Spieth, and chatted about politics. He mentioned that the Dallas City Council was probably moving some banking business to the City Bank of Dallas and that City Bank was coming on strong in the Dallas area.

I declined to comment on City Bank or the council and changed the subject to banking practices. I told him I was working a case and I needed information on banking practices and money, but I wanted the simple version.

He smiled and launched into his favorite topic. "First of all, banking is not what it used to be. It is now more complicated, more profitable and way more political. I'm just giving you my opinions and some people will disagree, so don't take what I'm telling you as the gospel according to Saint Bernanke."

He laughed at his joke, signaled for another martini, and continued. "So what happens is you take your $100,000 and deposit it into my bank in a saving account or certificate of deposit. My job is to pay you a small amount of interest and loan it out at a much larger rate of interest. The difference is the profit. Of course we have overhead, salaries, bonuses, an expensive building, auditors and so forth, but that is the basic idea."

He took another sip and said, "But it gets better because I can take the 100 grand you deposited and loan it out five or ten times, and earn more interest for the bank."

He must have seen my face get tight, so he clarified, "Yes, but it is totally legal. That's the way fractional reserve banking works and everyone does it. There is no problem unless too many people want to withdraw their money at the same time, which is called a bank run. We've had a few in this country and you probably heard about recent bank runs in England or Scotland. But the Federal Reserve always cranks up the printing presses and ships us more cash or digital money so we never run short."

He stopped to sip his martini and I jumped in, "So in effect you loaned out that 100 grand say 10 times and created from nothing 900 thousand bucks. Is that right?"

He looked at me like I was in Junior High. "Of course! That's how we make money, cover the overhead, and pay my bonuses. Another beer?"

I drained mine and said, "Sure." But I needed more information. "So how does a bank get in trouble?"

"There are lots of ways. The bank can loan out say $300,000 on a house, the market goes down, the house is only worth $175,000, the mortgage holder leaves town and mails the keys to the bank. We eat the loss. It happened a lot a few years ago. Or the bank can loan money to a business and it goes belly up. We expect a certain number of bankruptcies and business failures. It's built into our business model."

Fred drained his 2nd martini and signaled for a third. "There are other ways for the big banks to get in trouble. Suppose they are speculating in the giant casino that we call the stock, bond, or foreign exchange market. Maybe they bet wrong and lose a few hundred million bucks. It happens and sometimes a bank goes down, gets bought out, and we move on. It is no big deal unless hundreds of banks go down at the same time."

I noticed he was getting tense and a bit agitated. Had I hit a nerve? Maybe he needed high blood pressure meds. "But the real killer probably will be derivatives. Say a bank puts up ten million bucks and makes a billion dollar bet. The bet goes sour and all that leverage turns against the bank and they lose two hundred million bucks or more. It is nothing to JP Morgan but it might be significant to a smaller bank."

He signaled for number four. I drank my second beer and asked, "So I'm getting the impression that money sloshes around creating huge profits and losses. Banks create money out of nothing by loaning it into existence and leverage it with big bets on mortgages, business loans, derivatives, and other financial products. What backs all that money? I mean it has to be backed with gold or something, right?"

Fred looked at me like Hilda does when I ask a stupid question. "Gold has nothing to do with it. The Federal Reserve, the Treasury, and the banks manage the dollars, create more as needed, loan it into existence, and nobody worries about gold or backing. I mean it is backed by the full faith and credit of the US government and that is solid. What more could you want?"

Playing dumb I asked, "But what happens if people or global governments or businesses lose confidence in the mighty dollar?"

"Never happen! The dollar is solid and we've got the military to back it up. Some piss-ant country wants to stiff us by not taking dollars so we bomb them until they see the light. Ask Saddam Hussein what he thinks about not taking our dollars for his oil. See what I mean?"

"So we create more dollars every day, loan them out, keep it all moving, and prices gradually rise because there are more dollars in play?"

He answered, "That's about right. But who cares how many zeros are on the money if everybody has enough. Look at us, you're doing alright, I'm doing great. Who cares if a martini costs 8 bucks or 80 cents? Look, we have PhD economists running the show at the highest level. They are way smarter than both of us, and I trust them to keep the whole machine working."

He and Mr. Mystic would not get along. I could see that it was about time to move onto safer ground, like his golf swing, but before I did, I had to ask a couple more questions. "So really, we create more dollars every year, add to the debt, never repay it, and the economy keeps chugging along. Then we repeat the process. Isn't that a Ponzi scheme?"

I think he realized I finally understood. "Of course it is. Bernie Madoff had nothing on the Federal Reserve and the Treasury. The only difference is that our system is legal and he's in the slammer. Another beer?" He signaled for the waitress.

"But what about gold, Fort Knox and all that? Why isn't the money backed by gold anymore?"

He gave me the stupid school kid look again and said, "If the money is tied to gold, you can't expand the money supply, can't create massively more debt, can't afford wars and all those silly social programs, and my bonus shrinks to peanuts. Gold backed money is a bad idea whose time is gone, thank God." He emptied his martini glass and his eyes looked a bit glassy.

"But what if we went back to a gold standard?" I can be persistent.

"That's truly a stupid idea. To back most of the money in the system, not counting the derivatives and the dark money, you would have to price gold at $10,000 an ounce, or maybe $100,000 per ounce. Who knows? It would be some huge number and that is a very bad idea. Do not rock the boat, and we can keep this sucker running for another decade or so."

"You mean the system as we run it is not sustainable?"

"I didn't say that and the idea is preposterous. Say, I've got to be going. It was good chatting with you. I'll get the check. Hit 'em straight and long. Bye!"

He walked off, a little unsteady on his feet. He would be irritated with me for a week but in a few months it would all be forgotten, his bonus check would be safe, and maybe his golf handicap would be back down to a 7. Since it upset him I would never mention gold, the gold standard, or gold backing again.

I drove home and watched the Rangers lose 7 to 6 in the 9th inning. I thought about Ponzi schemes, and wondered why, if PhD economists were so smart, the system was so screwed up. No answers presented themselves so I went to bed.

Chapter 6

The next morning I got to the office about 9 am. Hilda was already hard at work. I told her, "You were right about the banking scam, but the banker I talked to last night told me it was business as usual."

"Did he mention the words Ponzi and scheme?"

"Actually, he did. What do you make of that?"

"Then he might have been telling the truth."

"By the way, I mentioned gold and backing the dollar with gold and he practically had a heart attack. I think that pushed him over the edge."

"My dad always said that gold was the enemy of bankers and particularly central bankers. He said if we had gold backing our money it would still be mostly honest money, not the fraudulent crap we use today. He also said that a lot of bankers, politicians, and economists would be out of a job, so don't expect it to happen anytime soon."

"Your dad sounds like Mr. Mystic."

Hilda smiled and looked pleased.

I told her, "I'm going to that other coin store you recommended. I'll be back in a few hours."

I found the paper Hilda had given me, looked at the address, remembered seeing the building, and drove in that direction. Traffic was heavy and people were cranky, or maybe it was just me. By the time I arrived, I was irritated at people, bankers, high prices, bad coffee, lying politicians, and just about everything.

I found a parking place and gave myself ten minutes to breathe and relax before I entered the coin store. My cranky mood would not win friends so I wanted it banished before I started asking questions.

The door was locked with an electronic gizmo. When a sales clerk saw me she buzzed me in. A pretty young woman asked if she could show me some silver eagles. I thought why not, and encouraged her.

"I'm Melissa and this is a 2014 Silver Eagle minted by the US government. I think it is one of the prettiest coins ever made. You may not have seen the St. Gaudens gold coins from over 100 years ago, but this Eagle is modeled after that classic design."

She passed the coin to me and I looked at it, turned it over, and felt the weight. I wondered how it would sound if I dropped it on the floor. "It is pretty. I see that it contains one ounce of silver. What does this coin cost?"

"The coin price varies with the price of silver. Today the silver price is about $16.00 per ounce so this coin costs about $19.00 and slightly less if you buy 100 at a time."

"So this is like a modern day silver dollar?" I wanted to hear her response.

"Well, yes and no. A silver dollar contained 0.77 ounces of silver and this coin contains one full ounce. A silver dollar could be 80 to 230 years old and will have some numismatic value, which is mostly determined by how rare that coin is."

I gave her a quizzical look. She opened a display case and brought out a coin in a sealed plastic case. "Let me show you an example. This is a silver dollar from the Carson City mint dated 1882. That was a small mintage year so this coin sells for almost $3,000 today. It might sell for twice that in a few years. But on average rare coins appreciate in value. Here, take a look at it, and note the grade shown there."

She pointed to something that said MS-65. I thought it was interesting that coins had grades and could be worth 3,000 times their face value.

"The MS-65 designation means that it is Mint State 65 condition, which is uncirculated. You can see that it has no wear and is almost as nice as when it left the mint some 135 years ago."

"So why don't we still use silver coins? I remember silver coins from my youth?"

She sighed and told me, "The price of silver went too high so they stopped minting silver coins and replaced them with silver colored coins that contained copper."

"Why did silver prices get too high to mint coins?"

"Oh, I have no idea but my manager would know. He lived through those years and can probably give you a good explanation. But you can see that silver prices have gone up considerably since they stopped minting silver coins in the 1960's, and they will go up more in the future. I suggest you purchase a tube of 20 coins, or maybe several tubes, and save them in anticipation of the government creating another massive inflation."

I thanked her and told her I would think about it. I asked if I could wander around and look at other coins. "Sure, call me if you want a closer look at anything."

It occurred to me that this was probably a typical coin store and that Mystic Coins was unusual. In fact, Mystic Coins had been downright strange.

I looked in display cases and saw silver coins from Canada, China, Australia and other countries. I saw a number of old coins from the US, such as silver dollars and half dollars from days gone by. I also saw gold coins, including the US Gold Eagle, the South African Krugerand, and the Canadian Maple Leaf. I liked the gold coins. They were beautiful and substantial and I wondered what they cost. I looked toward the back of the store and saw a sign that updated often. It listed spot prices for gold and silver. I assumed that was the base price and the store added a premium for the coin and for their profit.

I mumbled to myself, "I could like these coins. I see why Mrs. MacDougall had such fond memories of silver dollars."

Apparently the manager had been watching. He approached, stuck out his hand and said, "I'm George Clanton, manager of Dallas Rare Coin Investments."

We shook hands and I told him, "This is my first experience in a coin store. I see why people love these coins, old and new. They seem more real and substantial than the pieces of paper we use now."

George smiled and said, "Let me show you something interesting. This way."

He led me to a different section of the store that had paper money, not coins, on display. He removed a twenty dollar bill from a display case and carefully handed it to me. I noticed that it was protected with a plastic sleeve.

"Look carefully at this bill. You can see that it is a $20 bill, but note the words here. 'In gold coin payable to the bearer on demand.' Look at the year – 1930. These are collector's items, the government will not honor these as money anymore. But that's the point. Real gold was money then and it is money now, unlike this piece of paper. Gold was valuable then and is more valuable now. In fact gold is selling at about $1,200 per ounce today and someday it will be much higher. This paper bill is just paper. It has value only if another collector wants to buy it. Gold has value everywhere and always. Back then you often heard that the dollar is good as gold. You never hear that now."

I could hear him warming up for an impassioned sales pitch, so I tried to redirect it. "What about silver? Was it possible to exchange dollars for silver?"

He brought out another bill and I noticed that it said "Silver Certificate." I smiled and said, "I remember these." The date was 1928.

"Yes, at one time the US government would honor these and exchange them for silver. It took some effort and almost nobody did, but it was possible. "

I asked him, "So why did they stop making silver dollars? What happened to those marvelous old silver cartwheels?"

"The government borrowed and spent so much money that the dollar bought far less than a decade before. The prices for everything went sky high, including silver and gold, and the silver in a silver dollar was worth way more than a dollar. They had to quit minting silver coins."

I said sarcastically, "But the PhD bankers and economists were in charge. What happened?"

He looked skeptically at me and said, "I gave you the official story. But if you want to hedge your dollars against continued devaluation, buy some gold and silver coins. Both the old numismatic coins and the new bullion coins are good, and they will get priced higher, on average, every year."

I looked suspicious, so he showed me a chart of average silver prices. He pointed out $1.03 in 1960, $1.63 in 1971, and $16.39 in 1980. "But this $16.39 was an average price in 1980. The daily price went to $50 for a few minutes in January of 1980. Then the silver price crashed, like the stock market in 1929, down to $4.01 in 2001, and rallied back to $48.50 in 2011, and crashed again to under $15.00 in 2015. As you can see, silver prices jump around. But you know the old story, buy low, sell high. Silver prices are low in 2015. Maybe they will increase later in 2015, or maybe not until 2016 or 2017. All I know is that, on average, silver and gold are going much higher because the dollar and other currencies are printed to excess and that means devaluation of global currencies. Things will cost more."

"That part I understand." I had heard enough for the day. I thanked him and returned to Melissa and told her I wanted to buy five Silver Eagles. I gave her some green paper money and watched as she put five Eagles in a plastic tube.

I left the store feeling good.

Chapter 7

I greeted Hilda at 8:15 the next morning. She nodded and handed me a piece of paper with some ideas that might produce work for us. I thanked her and read the morning newspaper in my office. About ten minutes later I heard the bell ring and a man introduced himself to Hilda.

A moment later she brought him into my office and introduced him as Mr. John Winterstone. Hilda left, closed the door, and I shook his hand.

"Mr. Winterstone, what can I do for you?"

"I need a detective to follow my wife."

He looked sheepish and slightly ashamed, as if somehow it diminished him as a husband that he didn't know everything about his wife's life. He was young, and I had news for him about wives, but this was not the time. "Okay, tell me more."

"I think she might be having an affair, and I can't stand not knowing. I have to know for sure. Normally I'd say we had a good marriage and a good sex life and that nothing was wrong, but I can't say that."

He looked like he was in serious pain and I wanted to tell him it would be okay, and he was probably worried about nothing. But 30 some years in this business had taught me that if a husband thought his wife was having an affair, then she probably was. "So you want me to follow her, or what? Tell me why you are suspicious."

Once he started talking, he couldn't stop. I heard how they had been college sweethearts, how they both had good jobs, how he thought they were very much in love, and much more. "But every Thursday night my wife leaves the house and she won't tell me where she is going. She comes home, usually around midnight, looking happy, and tells me she loves me. Then she climbs into bed, snuggles in, and goes right to sleep. But I don't sleep because I'm worried my wife is screwing another man."

He paused, looked sad and dejected, and said, "I have to know. Can you follow her and tell me where she goes and who she meets?"

"I can, but why don't you follow her yourself. There is no need to hire me."

"Sensible, but I can't do that. It wouldn't be right. I can't snoop on her, but you can."

I didn't see the distinction but he did and that was what was important. I told him I would do it, named my daily rate plus expenses and he promptly agreed. He told me where they lived, her car and license number, her name, and gave me a picture of her. He asked me to discretely follow her, find out who she met, and report back to him on Friday morning. Today was Wednesday.

We agreed, shook hands, and he left looking five years younger and happier. I wanted to help him.

I told Hilda I was working on a case, left the office, and drove north to find his house. I stopped at a donut shop on the way and ate a pastry that cost me $1.50 but would have cost a dime several decades ago. Mrs. MacDougall had affected me. I drank expensive coffee and ate overpriced pastry and thought about Mrs. Winterstone and Mrs. MacDougall and what to do next.

About mid-way through my refill I had a plan for both. Mrs. Winterstone was easy. Locate her house, find out more about her, follow her tomorrow night, get pictures, make notes, call the husband on Friday, and give him the bad news.

The Mrs. MacDougall job was tougher. I had talked to a mysterious coin and bullion dealer, my banker friend, another coin dealer, and I had skimmed many books at the library. I still didn't know what to think about Mr. Mystic and his "alternate-Dallas" scenario. For the moment I had it mentally filed under, "don't understand, probably wacky, wait for more information, and don't overreact."

Mr. and Mrs. Winterstone lived in a very attractive home in a good neighborhood in north Dallas. The house appeared to be 3,000 square feet, built on a modest lot, well maintained, and encouraged the image of upper-middle class rising to bigger and better things in another decade. I was neither envious nor particularly interested. It was their dream, not mine.

On the way back to my office I stopped at my bank and asked a few questions at the customer service desk. My savings were guaranteed by the FDIC up to $250,000, which was considerably more than what was in my account, my money was earning 0.75% interest per year. I asked what would happen if the bank failed and was assured that it could never happen. Never is a long time so I pushed back and discovered that my money was actually a liability of the bank, and that I had entrusted my money with the bank, and they could do pretty much whatever they wanted. I was told not to worry, the bank was solid, there had never been a run on that bank, and the FDIC was guaranteeing all deposits.

I did not like the answers but assumed these were standard responses given to anyone who asks questions, and maybe the very pleasant customer service representative actually believed them. I asked her why the bank was paying so little interest on my account. I no longer called it my money, but my account. She said it was a market rate and the market had been low for years following the 2008 crash. I asked her what interest rate the bank charged on credit card balances. She smiled sweetly and told me 11.99% up to 21.99% depending upon my credit record. I asked her if those rates had gone down since the 2008 crash. She answered that they had changed very little but they also were market rates, and did I need anything else?

She had turned frosty when I asked about the bank's credit card rates because she had decided I was a trouble maker, while I saw myself as an informed customer.

"Thank you for your time. I truly appreciate your help."

"Certainly, Mr. Chandler. Anytime. Have a nice day."

She didn't care if I had a nice day, and her sincerity had dropped to zero. I was troubled for perhaps a quarter of a second by her disapproval. I no longer saw banks as before, and my new perspective made much more sense.

When I got back to the office I asked Hilda to find out everything she could on Mrs. Winterstone. I don't know how she does it, or where she goes, but Hilda could deliver information that surprised me. And I was the detective. I appreciated the irony.

Chapter 8

Thursday morning dawned bright and clear. My thinking was not clear. I doodled in the office drawing dollar signs, crude pictures of silver dollars, and a bar of silver that I had seen at Mystic Coins.

Then it occurred to me I was investigating a murder and I should approach it as such. I made notes on my yellow pad.

1) Silver had been money in the 1950's and before.
2) Deficit spending, politics, wars, corruption, and greed had poisoned silver money.
3) I was a simpleton when it came to global economics, money, and power politics, so there had to be much more I didn't understand, but I could see the broad outline of the murder.
4) Silver coins circulating as money were dead. I blamed President Johnson but that was mostly because I had despised him long before I met Mrs. MacDougall. However, his escalation in Vietnam and his social program spending had injected the poison into those beloved silver dollars.

5)   Now we had paper money that was based on a debt from the Federal Reserve. It was backed by faith and credit, not gold or silver.

6)   I could not see any value in the Federal Reserve, but the PhD's had assured us it was necessary. I'd file that one under "maybe."

7)   The bottom line was that silver dollars were real money and they were dead, paper money and digital money were nothing more than debt, and it all seemed backwards.

8)   Then it hit me! The paper dollars were pretend money, supported by dwindling faith in the dollar, and consequently the paper stuff bought less each year. Every five to ten years the pretend stuff was revalued closer to what it was really worth, and that was called a crash. We pretended stocks were worth more than they actually were, and later they crashed. Silver and gold had gone sky high and crashed after the 1980 peak.

9)   So pretend money buys less every decade, encourages delusional prices, occasionally crashes, and the PhD's tell us the paper stuff is better than real money. I wondered about the payoffs to the PhD's.

10) My BS detector was buzzing an alert regarding the PhD economists, funny money, and government reassurances.

11) My second insight was simple. The paper money, digital money, and unbacked debt paper were easier for the economists and the government to create and manipulate. Consequently they promoted it aggressively and discouraged gold and silver. Paper money was not better for the average citizen, but we were just collateral damage in their massive Ponzi scheme.

I reread my list, decided it made sense, but I still did not fully understand how and why silver dollars had been killed.

I leaned back in my chair and realized it sounded like a detective novel. The patriarch of the family, Doctor Silver Cartwheel, is wealthy and has raised two spoiled sons, call them banking and politics. They plot together and poison the old man, inherit all his wealth, and squander it on hot cars, airplanes, fighting, hookers, drugs, and booze.

I visualized Doctor Silver Cartwheel as a tall, gaunt, elderly gentleman with a kind face. He believed in moral values and lived his life with integrity and decency. Unfortunately his two sons were intelligent but undisciplined, and were always chasing easy money, fast women, drugs and booze.

Now I understood.

■■■

Hilda brought in her report on Mrs. Winterstone. So Hilda claimed, and I had no doubt she was 99% correct, Mrs. Winterstone had graduated from the University of Texas, met her future husband in Austin, married a few years out of college, and currently lived in North Dallas. She worked as a commercial property insurance agent, made a good living, and seemed to be a good citizen. There was nothing to suggest marital unhappiness or extra-marital affairs. I would discover her secret in a few hours.

At 6:30 pm I was parked half a block from their home, watching for her garage door to open. The neighborhood was relatively quiet, a few cars came and went, a couple of children were playing in their front yard, and I saw two teenage boys tossing a football back and forth. One threw a tight spiral a long way. I thought quarterback in High School.

Ten minutes before 7 pm Judy Winterstone backed out of her garage, turned the opposite direction and drove down her street. I discretely followed her, keeping considerable distance between us. In a few minutes she took the freeway onramp and headed south into Dallas. I followed more closely to avoid losing her.

Mrs. Winterstone took a downtown exit, skillfully negotiated the traffic, drove another ten blocks and entered an underground parking garage. I had to make a decision – follow her into the garage and risk being spotted, or park on the street and hope to see her as she emerged.

I thought for a moment and followed her into the garage. She made three turns and parked. I passed her, made another turn, and parked. I quickly walked back to her level and realized I had missed her. Fortunately I saw the elevator door closing and assumed she was taking the elevator to street level.

I followed and emerged a minute behind her, looked around, and spotted her waiting for a light at the corner. I watched her cross and turn left at the sidewalk, and right at the next intersection. As she rounded the corner I ran into the street, dodged traffic, heard several horns, and reached the corner a few seconds later. She walked half a block and entered a doorway. It was not the section of town for hotels and sexual liaisons.

I carefully noted the doorway she had entered and approached it cautiously. The sign above the door said, "St. Vincent Homeless Shelter."

I dismissed the theory that she was having an affair, peered into the window, and saw what looked like a shelter. There were old and young people sitting, talking and eating. I saw white, black, Asian and Hispanic men and women drinking coffee, sitting, standing in line, and a few passed out or sleeping on the floor.

It looked like a shelter, not a rendezvous for an affair. I wandered up and down the street for 15 minutes, watched the foot traffic go in and out and saw nothing special. Mrs. Winterstone had not left the building. I needed more information.

I entered the building feeling overdressed and was ignored by almost everyone. Apparently I did not stand out as much as I thought. I looked around, walked back to the food line, and saw Mrs. Winterstone serving potatoes and corn to a long line of hungry and appreciative people. She piled potatoes and corn on plastic plates and passed them to the next person who added meat. She looked happy and spoke to many of the people in line. I now knew what she did but not why she wanted it kept secret from her husband, which was none of my business. I removed a tiny camera from a pocket, discretely took several no flash pictures of her in the serving line, and was about to leave when an old man came up to me and said, "You're new here. I ain't seen you before."

"Yes, I just saw the building and wandered in. Looks like it does good things for people."

"Yeah, and the people working here are the best. You see them behind the food. That's Mrs. Horton, Mrs. Stone, and Mr. Robinson. They been here a while and they're nice. You take care. I'm getting in line."

He entered the food line and I walked back to my car. It would be an easy report to Mr. Winterstone the next morning. Like Mrs. MacDougall, Mr. Mystic, paper money, and silver dollars, there was more to the story.

I went home and slept well feeling good about the universe.

Chapter 9

The next morning I called Mr. Winterstone and gave him the news. I could almost see his smile and relief when he heard that his wife was volunteering in a homeless shelter and not having an affair. He seemed to understand why she wanted to keep it a secret and I didn't press the subject. I offered to send him a picture but he declined. I told him I'd send a bill and he said he would be happy to pay it. I felt like I had done a good deed for the day.

I thought about visiting another coin store, or going back to the library, or asking Hilda to do some magic with her computer, but all of those felt hollow. I understood the broad outlines of the murder of Doctor Silver Cartwheel but I had not answered my questions about motive, means and opportunity.

I doodled while I waited for inspiration, relaxed and tuned out for a few minutes. I heard a door slam down the hall and that brought me back to present day. I looked at my doodles and saw that I had drawn five silver eagles but the last three had crude images of Mr. Mystic instead of the St. Gaudens model. That settled it for me; I needed to visit Mr. Mystic.

I told Hilda where I was going and she smiled like she had been waiting for me to announce what she knew I needed to do. I would not want to run my office without Hilda, but she could be annoying, especially when she is right.

I drove to Mystic Coins, buzzed in, and was immediately greeted by the same lady I had previously met. I asked her if Mr. Mystic was available but not five seconds later he emerged from his office and greeted me. Did everyone know what I was going to do before I knew?

He invited me into his office and said, "You look troubled. What can I do?"

I sat down and tried to put my thoughts in order. I didn't do very well but he waited patiently. Finally I managed to say, "You gave me perspective on silver and got me thinking about banks, the nature of money, paper currencies, gold backing and inflation. I understand that spending too much on war and social programs along with a generous dose of graft and corruption caused silver prices to become so expensive that the government could no longer mint silver coins. But when I write it down or tell the story to myself, it sounds hollow and simple. There has to be more. If you have the time, I'm ready to hear more."

He looked at me for a long time and made his decision. "You are correct, you need more information and more perspective to understand the issues. Before we get started would you like a cup of coffee?"

I told him I was fine and waited.

"I could pick any number of places to start and I wish there was an easy place to say it all began here, but there isn't. Paper money was invented in China and we could start there. Of course it failed, just like it has practically everywhere else. The Bank of England was created in 1694 and was one of the first central banks. I think Sweden actually had an earlier bank but it matters not. The Federal Reserve, our central bank, was modeled after the English Central Bank and it was started in 1913. That is not the only place to start but since it is our central bank and they control the currency we might as well call that ground zero for the murder of honest money."

I thought to myself, "My, he gets right to it. What comes next?"

Mr. Mystic waved his hand and said, "Not many people have seen the media room but I think we should start there. He stood and we walked to another locked room labeled 'Media Room.'"

Inside he turned on a projector and said, "I have slides that I created for another presentation. I'll show them to you." He fiddled with a projector, pressed some buttons and I settled into a comfortable chair. The lights dimmed and I relaxed.

He brought up the first slide and said, "This is a good place to start. What is the most important commodity in the world? I know, it is a rhetorical question. The answer is crude oil. We need energy, plastics, chemicals, and thousands of other items, all made from crude oil directly or indirectly. So look at this graph of crude oil and silver prices back to 1913. You can see silver prices on the left axis and crude oil prices on the right axis."

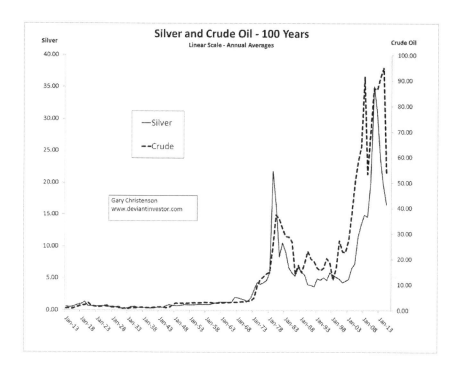

I studied the chart for a moment but the message was clear. Prices had very slowly increased from 1913 until the early 1970's. After that they took off like a rocket and practically went straight up.

"You can see the drastic price increases in the early 1970's. You can blame the Arab countries or the decline in US oil production and both are correct. But in my opinion the real issue was the US government created and spent too many dollars, and the rest of the world got tired of accepting devalued and recently printed dollars in exchange for real products. President Nixon refused to exchange US dollars for gold after August 1971 and that, in my opinion, really kicked the inflation and loss of confidence into high gear. Prices doubled and kept increasing. Crude oil went from a buck or so to about $40 and silver moved upward from about a dollar to over $50 in January 1980. The graph shows a high price in the low $20's for 1979, but that is because I've graphed the annual average prices, not the spike high in January of 1980."

He was on a roll and I kept my mouth shut.

"Look at the graph one more time. You saw it on a linear scale. Now look at this log scale graph." He flashed another graph on the screen and it looked like the same graph but compressed.

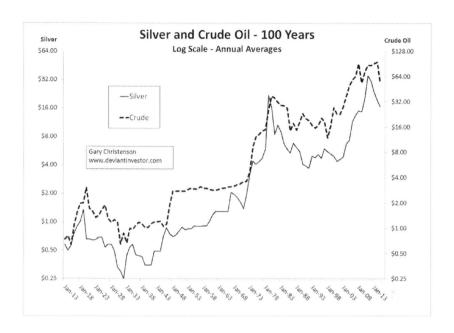

"A log scale graph compresses price movements so the move from $1 to $2 takes the same space as a move from $20 to $40. They are both doubles. We use log scale graphs when there are huge price multiples involved. Now look at those lines for silver and crude oil prices. Remember, these are the average prices for each year so they have much of the price volatility smoothed out."

He used a pointer to focus my attention. I felt like I was in a high school math class. "The point of a log scale graph is to see that prices flop around, but on average they double every 10 years or so. Now why do you think that is?"

"They keep spending and printing money and so the money buys less." I sounded confident but I wasn't totally certain.

"Correct! Now look at this graph. It is the same data but smoothed with several years averaged together to take out even more price volatility. The major point is that crude oil and silver prices move together, on average, since they are both commodities and are both affected by the declining value of the dollar."

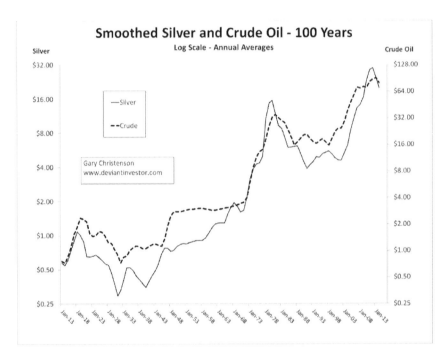

"Next, look at this graph of the official national debt of the United States." He put up another slide that had a line that looked like it was climbing an incredibly steep mountain. "As you can see, the debt has gone bonkers – over $18 Trillion and counting. Imagine if you ran your finances like the US government runs theirs."

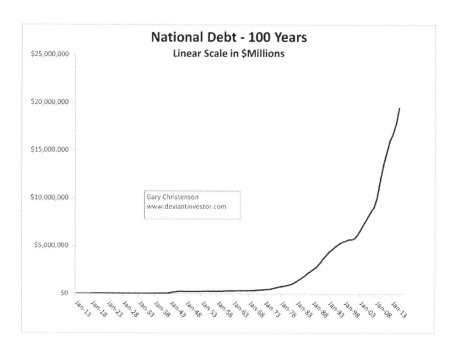

I imagined going to a bank for a loan every year, then going to the bank twice a year for a loan, and eventually going to ten different banks every month to procure loans. I knew it would not work for long.

"This is the same information. It shows over 100 years of national debt on a log scale. You can see that the total debt in 2015 is around $18 Trillion, or an 18 followed by 12 zeroes. The debt keeps climbing and has increased about 10,000 times its 1913 level."

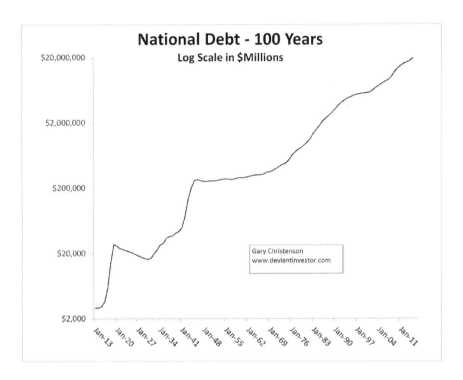

National Debt - 100 Years

Log Scale in $Millions

Gary Christenson
www.deviantinvestor.com

He paused to let me think and asked, "Do you see the connection between increasing debt, a weaker dollar, and increasing silver and crude oil prices?"

I hesitated and said, "Yes, but is the debt the cause or the effect from something else? And what about population increase? We have many more people now than in 1913."

"Excellent questions! I'll get to both in a few minutes. For now let's agree that debt has increased say 9% per year, on average, since 1913. Silver and crude oil prices have increased similarly but not quite as rapidly. Let's focus on the post 1971 period for more clarity."

He paused to catch his breath and sat down across from me. "In the late 1960's the US government was spending money aggressively and still operating under the Bretton Woods Agreement in which the dollar was pegged to a gold price and other currencies were pegged to the dollar. It was an uneasy truce until other countries realized that the US was printing the dollars to pay for the Vietnam War but still expecting foreign countries to value them the same as all other dollars. So the other countries did what you would expect. They demanded gold in exchange for depreciating paper dollars. The official US hoard of gold went down from 20,000 tons to under 10,000 tons and the politicians and bankers were worried. They had no intention of balancing their budget or reducing spending, and they couldn't allow all their gold to leave the country, so they made a decision."

He paused as if he was begging me to jump in. I had no clue so I just sat there.

"In 1971 President Nixon cancelled the agreement with other nations, subsequently refused to redeem dollars for gold, and let the dollar float in value against gold and other currencies. In other words, as we printed more dollars the value of each dollar went down and the price of gold went up. Prior to 1971 they had tried to hold the dollar price of gold at $35 and then $42 per ounce. Note that the price of gold is now about $1,200 so you can see that dollars have lost considerable value compared to gold since 1971."

"Nixon did what most politicians do. He lied and blamed others. He claimed that suspending conversion of dollars for gold was temporary and blamed speculators. Both statements were lies but he was the President. The point is not that politicians are liars but that the prices for silver and crude oil took off after 1971 and the national debt has gone parabolic since then. Look at the log scale graphs of silver and crude oil prices since 1971."

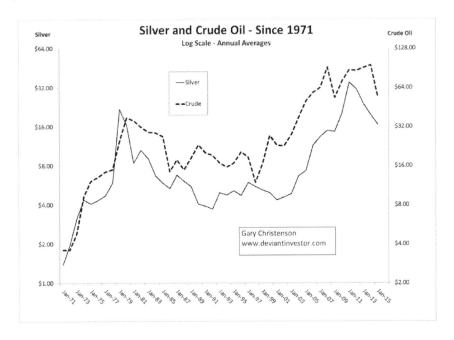

He flashed another graph on the screen. The dime pastry that cost me a buck and a half a couple days ago made more sense.

"You are correct that the population has increased since 1913 and that had a small influence on debt. But let's take the national debt and divide it by the population of the US so we see the increase in debt per person. I put it on a log scale chart and you can see that it increased consistently at about 7% per year since 1971."

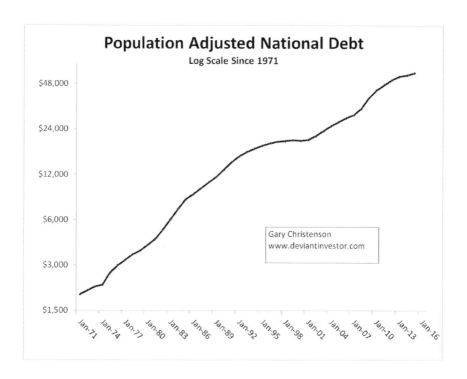

Population Adjusted National Debt

Log Scale Since 1971

Gary Christenson
www.deviantinvestor.com

I looked at him with a question on my face and asked, "So debt goes up and up forever. But isn't there a limit? It doesn't make sense that debt can increase forever."

"Of course debt can't increase forever, but the politicians and bankers have successfully increased debt since 1913. Don't expect them to stop now. Imagine all the corporations and politicians whose wealth and power depend upon selling the 'more debt and more spending' story to each other. My guess is that even the stupid politicians know it can't last forever, but all they care about is the next election and how many payoffs they collect along the way. Besides, it has worked for 100 years, why not another 10 or 20?"

He looked sad, like he knew what would happen but didn't want to pop my delusional bubble. I didn't understand modern finance but I did understand delusions and lying to yourself.

"Okay, I get it. Don't rock the boat, keep the money flowing to the bankers, the politicians, the military, the pharmaceutical companies and hundreds of others, and make sure those donations flow into congress. Let the PhD economists tweak the system, lie to each other, and pray the whole mess doesn't crash at our feet."

"You said it, not me, but I agree. Now look at this final chart of population adjusted national debt, and smoothed crude oil and silver prices since 1971 on a log scale. Generally speaking silver and crude oil prices move together and both increase with the population adjusted national debt. But remember, debt is huge and increases consistently. Silver and crude oil prices rally far too high and then crash to insane lows and then they do it again. Maybe the Arabs are restricting the supply of oil like in the 1970's, maybe people are scared about inflation like in the late 1970's, or maybe they think the only place to invest is the stock market, like in the 1990's. It does not matter as people will always find reasons and excuses. But the bottom line is that the US government spends far more than it collects in revenues, we know the Federal Reserve will create the extra dollars, those new dollars devalue all existing dollars in the system, so prices for stocks, automobiles, insurance, food, medical care, college tuition, and most everything else rise along with the increase in the money supply. If necessary the politicians lie, find someone to blame, or start a war."

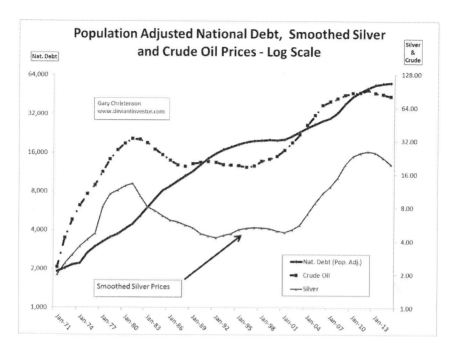

Population Adjusted National Debt, Smoothed Silver and Crude Oil Prices - Log Scale

He paused and I absorbed it for a minute or so. Finally I said, "So we can pretty well guarantee that the population will increase, the debt will increase even faster, and the dog and pony shows in Washington, London, Paris, and Tokyo will continue borrowing and spending. Silver used to sell for under a buck an ounce and now it is 16 times higher, the stock market is many times higher than it used to be, and the dollar purchases only a fraction of what it did 50 years ago. It sounds like a gigantic money printing and spending machine that is enabled and encouraged by everyone."

I thought about it some more and said, "If all that is true, the price of silver and crude oil must increase a lot more, maybe not tomorrow or even next year, but certainly in five or ten years."

Mr. Mystic shook his head indicating that yes, he agreed, and I continued, "But I still think you can't increase debt forever and no government, system or country lasts forever. It looks to me like the financial system is in trouble. It reminds me of partying on the Titanic the night before it hit the iceberg. It is a runaway train heading for the massive barrier at the end of the line, but nobody has noticed the engineer jumped off a long way back."

"I agree with you, but don't forget that this train has been running down the tracks for a long time and it might be years before it hits the wall."

"The whole thing is sobering and depressing and I need some time. Mr. Mystic, as usual, you have been wonderful, even if your message was discouraging. But I need to think about what you have shown me."

I stood to leave, shook his hand and walked out. I was in a daze and I realized I might not be safe driving home so I walked around the block a few times to clear my head.

I drove home early, called Hilda and told her I wasn't coming back to the office, and took a nap. It had been a hard day.

Chapter 10

I arrived before 9am, said hello to Hilda and would have gone to my office but Hilda asked, "How did it go with Mr. Mystic yesterday?"

I groaned and sat in one of my outer office chairs and thought about what he had said. I didn't want to spend an hour telling her, but it was complicated. "He showed me graphs of silver prices, crude oil prices, and the national debt back to 1913. What he said seems obvious but nobody ever thinks of it. We are too busy living and working to see the slow destruction of our money as the governments of the world take on more and more debt."

Hilda asked me, "Do you think the destruction of our money is intentional, or is it caused by stupidity, incompetence, or ordinary greed?"

"Hmmmm, a fair question." I thought for a moment and said, "I think we have highly intelligent people making decisions."

I stopped because Hilda gave me a "You have got to be kidding" look and rolled her eyes in disgust.

I quickly clarified, "No, not the morons we supposedly elect to public office, I'm talking about the billionaires and power-brokers behind the scenes who give the orders to the puppets that make speeches on prime time television."

Hilda smiled. I had temporarily redeemed myself. "I think the truly powerful people know exactly what they are doing as they increase their power and wealth at the expense of their countries and citizens. It is the same here as in Japan, ancient Rome, and modern Europe. But for the rest of the politicians and business leaders, I don't know. I'm guessing a mixture of greed, incompetence, short sighted thinking, and utter stupidity."

I paused, thought for a moment, and added, "What is equally bad is that we, as citizens of the world, put up with it. Nothing will change until we act differently, and based on what I hear on television, read in the newspapers, and see on the streets, it might be a long time."

Hilda said, "So what about silver?"

"In simple terms, silver prices increase along with the prices of everything else as we increase the quantity of money in circulation because governments spend too much money, way more than their revenues, and borrow the rest."

Hilda commented, "A ticket to a disaster. A runaway train. A house of cards. A guaranteed crash coming. A reckoning will occur. Have I missed any?"

"I think that about covers it. So how do you stay happy?"

"I look at what is real for my family, I think for myself, manage my own affairs and ignore the rest. Life is simpler that way, not easier, but simpler. If you want easy, take drugs, drink alcohol, believe the politicians, and watch daytime television."

"Thanks. I have work to do." I hid in my office for a while thinking about what I had learned at Mystic Coins and felt mildly irritated with Hilda.

About an hour later I heard the bell, waited, and shortly thereafter Hilda announced a Mr. Brian Morrison. The name sounded vaguely familiar. He entered and looked intense, intelligent, and capable. Mr. Morrison had a full head of wavy hair, a hard face with several laugh lines, ten extra pounds on an athletic frame, and wore an expensive suit. I guessed upper management and wealthy.

He stuck his hand out and said, "Hi, I'm Brian Morrison. Call me Brian. Can we chat privately?"

Hilda took the hint, closed the door and went back to work. I shook his hand, encouraged him to sit, and leaned back in my chair. "What can I do for you?"

"You come highly recommended as smart, discrete, and willing to keep your mouth closed, which is what I need. Should I explain further?"

He was a no-nonsense guy with troubles. Based on the stress showing on his face and in his voice, I guessed big troubles. "I do my best and I have never seen any value in shooting my mouth off about other people's business. So, I might be the person you want, depending on what's troubling you. Maybe you could give me a quick summary and then we can decide if you should go into more detail or go elsewhere."

He smiled and must have liked my equally direct approach. "I run a major financial firm. We specialize in mergers, acquisitions, and take-overs. Information is sensitive, time-critical, and immensely valuable. I can't afford to have that information leaked to competitors or targets."

He looked at me to determine if I was following him. "I understand so far. Please continue."

"The problem is I have a leak. I don't know who, where or how, and it has already cost me a seven figure commission. I have a deal working that could net an even larger commission and I'm afraid I'll lose it if someone leaks the information or somehow the information is stolen."

He looked exasperated and continued. "I already had the computer hot-shots look through my business, computers, phones, internet, and email and they found absolutely nothing. I figure the next step is the old-fashioned way, your way."

I admit it gave me some pleasure to realize that the modern hot-shot programmers and digital sleuths had found squat, and now he was asking an old dinosaur like me for help. I thought for 30 seconds and explored as many angles as I could with what little I knew. Finally I told him, "Okay, I can work for you on this. I need $700 per day plus expenses but I offer no guarantees. It sounds like a tough problem and it worries me that the other guys found nothing."

"Your $700 a day plus expenses is fine. I'll add a $25,000 bonus if you solve my problem within a month. This leak is killing my business and giving me an ulcer. You find my leak and I'll make certain you are well compensated."

I didn't like the job but I did like the challenge and the money. We talked for two more hours, I made pages of notes, and after an hour he looked more relaxed. I was overwhelmed and needed time to think. Mr. Morrison was intelligent, capable and had run a tight ship for years. There were no new employees and nothing obviously different. It would take time, some good detective work, and luck.

We shook hands and he left. I read my notes three more times, thought about ways to approach the problem, and at 4:30 called it a day. I went home and watched the Rangers blow a 7-4 lead in the 9th, rally back, and finally win with a walk-off homer in the 13th.

At the end of 13 innings I was tired but my inspiration had kicked in. I knew what I had to do the next day.

Chapter 11

ZASTROW'S DINER
THE HOME OF GOOD EATS

Plate Lunches . .	40c & 50c
All Pies, per slice . . .	15c
Pie-ala-mode . . .	20c
Coffee and Doughnuts . .	10c
Ice Cream, plain . . .	10c
Chocolate Sundae . . .	15c

S A N D W I C H E S

Virginia Baked Ham . .	20c
Toasted Cheese . . .	20c
Western Sandwich . .	20c
Ham and Cheese . . .	25c
Coney Island Hot Hogs .	10c
Hamburger	15c
Egg Sandwich . . .	10c
American Kraft Cheese . .	15c
Home Made Chili . . .	20c
Potato Salad	10c
Baked Beans . . .	10c
All Soups, per bowl . . .	15c
Ice Cold Pop . 5c Tomato Juice . 10c	

I said hello to Hilda the next day and she asked, "Are you going to Mystic Coins today?"

How did she know that was my plan? "Yes, how did you know?"

"I figured you would alternate jobs and yesterday was Mr. Morrison so today would be Mystic Coins." She smiled sweetly and looked pleased with herself. She irritated me.

"I'm going to see him in an hour or so. In the meantime, see what you can find out about Mr. Brian Morrison and his merger and acquisition business." I escaped to my office, my notes, and my morning newspaper.

An hour and a half later I entered Mystic Coins, said hi to the same lady, and before I could even ask about Mr. Mystic, she said, "He's expecting you and asked that you go back to his office." Hilda and the Mystic Coins people must be working together with a pipeline into my brain. Call it intuition.

I walked back and before I reached his office Mr. Mystic emerged, greeted me, shook my hand, and I felt a warm tingle from head to toe. This was strange and getting stranger.

He told me that he had spoken to Mrs. MacDougall. "She told me you were an unusual man, a little hard-headed, but otherwise quite pleasant and competent. She wanted me to give you the full treatment. Interested?"

Like I said, it was strange and getting stranger. What was the full treatment? It sounded like an extra-special massage or a total immersion mud-bath.

He beckoned to me and said, "This way." We walked down a hallway and arrived at another locked door labeled "Archive Room." He unlocked it with a key and a digital code and we entered. I felt like I was revisiting an episode of the "Twilight Zone" from decades ago. I also felt another tingle on the back of my neck. Maybe it was caused by low blood sugar but I didn't think so.

We entered the room, he pointed to a chair in the front row, about 10 feet from a large screen mounted on the wall. It looked like a flat screen television but considerably thicker. There were cables running to a large box placed a few feet in front of the screen. The box was about six feet wide, at least three feet high and another four feet deep. Mr. Mystic walked up and patted the box as if it were a beloved antique car or a beautiful sculpture. "This box provides the special power to run this viewing machine. I call it my 'Nothing Box' because nothing you can see goes in but power comes out."

I looked skeptical and he continued, "Yes, I know. That violates the laws of thermodynamics and physics as we currently know them. But there are several hundred of these boxes in operation right now, all around the world. Every central bank uses a 'Nothing Box' to create their currencies out of nothing. The Federal Reserve created over $16 Trillion from nothing in new currency, swaps, loans, guarantees and whatever after the 2008 crisis. The Japanese central bank has created untold trillions of yen, and it continues every day. A 'Nothing Box' makes the process easier. But it can also generate a special type of power as it does here."

I know I looked skeptical since this was beyond strange. Creating money out of nothing was possible, but producing power out of nothing just did not work for me, and I wasn't buying the story. Mrs. MacDougall had called me 'hard-headed' and this was a good example of why I was hard-headed. These make something out of nothing boxes couldn't be real. It had to be a fantasy.

Mr. Mystic said patiently, "It created billions of dollars back in the hey-day of savings and loans but I've had other uses for it since then. And yes, I know you don't believe a word I'm saying but give it a chance and I'll convince you."

He sounded sincere and I wanted to believe him, but something from nothing and violating the laws of physics were too much. Then I had an ugly thought. The banks created money from nothing, as per my discussion with Fred the banker. Mr. Mystic had also convinced me on that point. Maybe the 'Nothing Box' was fantastic only because it was unfamiliar to me. How would my grandfather back in the year 1899 have responded if I had shown him a baseball game on a 65 inch color television? He would have told me it was impossible, even as he watched it.

I was confused and bewildered, and I felt another tingle on the back of my neck.

Mr. Mystic went on as if six impossible things before lunch were normal. "Now, sit back, relax, and enjoy the show. You will see things that few human beings have ever seen. This is a remote viewing machine powered by the 'Nothing Box' and it will amaze you."

Now it was remote viewing. That sounded like a camera that took video from someplace a long way away, like in Paris at the Eiffel Tower. Okay, maybe that wasn't impossible. I had heard Hilda talk about web cams.

"Show me." I sounded harsh but he ignored my attitude.

"Pick a date from your childhood that you remember well. You could choose a birthday party, a first date, or some special occasion."

I thought for a moment and said, "My 7th birthday was special because my parents and my grandparents were there, and they gave me my first bicycle. My dad brought it out from behind the house after I blew out the candles on the cake. It was August 3, 1959." I felt so nostalgic that I forgot to be skeptical.

"Okay, I'll set the machine for August 3, 1959, here in Dallas, for say 4 pm. Is that correct?"

"Make it Denton, Texas and about 5 pm." I sounded like I believed this nonsense.

Mr. Mystic fiddled with dials and buttons, the screen came alive but filled with static and visual trash. About 30 seconds later the picture clarified and zoomed in toward the house where I had been raised. It was a tiny two bedroom house in Denton that had made my parents proud. It wasn't much but my dad owned it and had worked hard to pay off the mortgage. I grew up there and had fond memories of the house, playing baseball nearby, and going to school down the street.

A moment later the scene changed and I could see this blond haired kid, my parents, and my grandparents. The kid was me and my parents and grandparents looked young again. Call me blown away. My mouth dropped open and I leaned forward in my seat. I watched the birthday party on the screen, saw this little kid blow out seven candles and my dad retrieve a brand new bicycle from behind the house. The kid jumped up and down in excitement and ran to the bicycle.

This could not be happening, yet I was watching it. This was way stranger than a "Nothing Box."

I must have looked dazed. Mr. Mystic asked me, "Now are you convinced?"

"I'm convinced that you did something pretty amazing but I don't understand it."

"We don't have enough time to explain how this works for you to understand it. Just accept it. If you are still skeptical, give me another special date."

I thought for a moment and picked twenty days after my 18th birthday. It was special because that was the date I reported to the draft induction station. They had shipped me to Vietnam a few months later. I remembered it as a turning point in my life for lots of reasons that I don't want to discuss.

Mr. Mystic did his magical thing with the dials and the next image that popped up was a sterile building filled with young boys walking in their underwear herded along by uniformed soldiers. I recognized the building and one of the boys – me. My stomach tightened and I gripped the chair remembering what had happened next.

"Okay, I'm convinced. Shut it off and don't show me any more from that building." The screen went blank.

Mr. Mystic asked me, "Are you ready for a short trip through history to learn more about silver?"

I was glad to get out of the draft induction station and said, "Sure, show me silver history."

The screen changed and an image slowly appeared. It was dark and grainy and lacked the clarity of the images from my 7th birthday party. Gradually I realized it was a mine and men were digging with crude tools.

"This is ancient Rome and you are looking at a silver mine. It's not clear because the image is over 2,000 years ago. Notice the crude tools, minimal light, the whip marks on the backs of the men, and the armed soldiers. They used slaves to do the work. It was brutal and those slaves had a wretched life."

I watched for a few minutes and said, "Okay, I've had enough. Silver was wealth and they mined it with slaves. What's next?"

"Next is a mine from Colorado in the 1870's near Silverton." The screen reset and gradually became clear. The mine looked dark and dangerous, but the miners had better tools, rail cars to move the ore, and I saw no soldiers. They weren't slaves, just workers. It was a big improvement.

"Next is a grocery store in Dallas in 1913, before the Federal Reserve was created. Watch how the customers paid for their groceries."

He adjusted the machine and soon I saw a group of people dressed in antique clothes in a store that looked nothing like a modern supermarket. Much of the food was in bulk and the prices seemed unreal. A bag of potatoes was a dime, apples were a few cents per pound, and a loaf of bread was a nickel. I watched a man in a bowler hat pay for several boxes of groceries with one silver dollar, a quarter, and 3 pennies.

Times had changed. Mr. Mystic shifted the scene to the back room and I saw a pasty faced man in a green eyeshade counting money. In front of him were stacks of silver dollars, a 5 dollar gold piece, two $10 gold eagles, and one $20 gold double eagle. The gold and silver coins were shiny and occasionally gleamed in the light. Some green paper money was stacked beside the gold and silver money.

He said, "A $20 dollar gold piece was a large amount of money back then. It might represent the wage for two weeks of work for a shop clerk."

I thought about $700 per day that I had quoted Mr. Morrison and wondered if the money had really lost that much value. I'd save the question for another time. But I was impressed seeing all those groceries purchased for a little more than one silver dollar and I was amazed at the stacks of real gold and silver next to the paper bills.

He took me through a few more events in US history. I saw President Roosevelt sign the executive order that authorized the US government to confiscate gold in excess of five ounces owned by private citizens. The government paid $20.00 in paper money for each confiscated $20.00 gold double eagle, or a little less than $21.00 per ounce of gold. Soon thereafter the government revalued confiscated gold at $35.00 per ounce. That partially explained why some people hated Roosevelt. He ran the machine forward to President Johnson and the Vietnam era. My stomach got tight watching lying politicians, protest marches, body bags, choppers, napalm, bombs and rice paddies. Next was President Nixon's speech where he announced that the US was breaking its promise to the rest of the world to redeem dollars with gold bullion. He said it was only temporary and blamed the speculators. I knew that was garbage.

He finished with a scene where people were buying gold and silver in January of 1980 when the price of gold had jumped hundreds of dollars per ounce in a few months, and silver had gone from under $10 to over $40 in a few weeks. He explained that inflation was killing their savings and people had lost confidence in dollars and were desperate to buy anything that would protect the value of their money.

"After the craziness in early 1980, the bankers crushed inflationary expectations, crashed gold and silver prices and the economy improved. The stock market boomed while gold and silver prices languished for the next 20 years. They further suppressed gold prices by selling vaulted gold, which the bankers called leasing. Also, the government continued liquidating a huge stockpile of more than a billion ounces of US government silver and that helped crush silver prices. They desperately wanted to avoid a repeat of the late 1970s where people had lost confidence in the dollar, the government, and the Federal Reserve."

Mr. Mystic looked at me, saw that I was overwhelmed, and asked, "Have you had enough for today?"

I shook my head for yes, and he shut down the machine and signaled for me to come with him. He asked an assistant for a pot of coffee and we sat in his office and drank coffee until I felt normal again.

"Thanks for a most interesting afternoon. I suspect you have more to show me, but I've had enough for today."

I slowly walked out and drove to my favorite 1950's diner for lunch. It had already been a long day.

Chapter 12

Lincoln Park, Chicago around 1900

I checked with Hilda when I returned to my office and she handed me her 11 page report on Mr. Morrison. I told her thanks and closed my office door. I didn't need to work on Mr. Morrison at this moment. What I needed was more perspective on silver and to think about what I had seen.

First, the experience with Mr. Mystic had been incredible. I didn't understand what remote viewing was or how Mr. Mystic had done it, but the vision of my seven year old birthday party had convinced me it was real. That made alternate-Dallas more plausible, but I still didn't understand. I reminded myself that I didn't understand how a telephone or an automobile ignition worked either, but I used both. Learning the big picture from Mr. Mystic was much more important than a detailed understanding of what happened inside the phone, ignition, or "Nothing Box." I accepted it and moved on.

Second, I did not understand a "Nothing Box" but clearly banks created currency from nothing so I had an easier time believing it than understanding how I could have seen a 2,000 year old Roman silver mine on what looked like a television screen.

Third, I believed the grocery store from a hundred years ago. It looked real and was consistent with what little I knew about groceries and prices from long ago.

Fourth, it was clear to me that Doctor Silver Cartwheel, aka silver dollar coins, had been poisoned and killed by government spending, central banks, greed, war, and politicians. That was easy to believe and understand.

Fifth, I needed more information on silver. Specifically, how much was mined each year, what was it worth in dollars, and how much silver existed in vaults? Hilda would find out for me if I asked her.

Sixth, it was time to meet with Mrs. MacDougall. I called her, left a message, and knew we would meet when the time was right.

I asked Hilda to do more silver research while I read through her report on Mr. Morrison. It was interesting, comprehensive, and gave me no immediate ideas.

Fifteen minutes later Mrs. MacDougall returned my call. We chatted for a few minutes and finally she said, "Mr. Chandler, why don't you have lunch with me at my club tomorrow? They have wonderful food, privacy, and a beautiful setting. I'll leave word for the gate and restaurant staff that you are my guest. Please arrive around 11:30 am."

The Colonial Dallas Country Club is exclusive. I asked Hilda what it cost to join and she smiled at me like I was so naïve.

"You can't just join. You have to be invited and accepted. I think the initiation fee is around $100,000 but it might be twice that. Are you interested in membership?"

"I'll pass. Ask me in ten years." She smiled and went back to work.

I returned to the Morrison file but couldn't get Mrs. MacDougall and Mr. Mystic out of my mind. The remote viewing machine still troubled me but I couldn't see any real difference between a remote viewing machine and a color TV, except that we all have color televisions. My grandfather didn't have a color TV and he would have thought they were equally impossible.

Besides, wasn't time just another dimension that had something to do with quantum wormholes? Years ago I had read an article about physics and black holes and time warps but I didn't understand it any more than I understood a computer, a color television, a cell phone, a remote viewing machine or a "Nothing Box."

I started day-dreaming about remote viewing machines and finding out the truth about the Kennedy assassination, the 9-11 tragedy, and dozens of other events about which I suspected politicians had lied. It occurred to me that remote viewing machines would be top secret and restricted, and few people would know about them. Truth is a precious commodity and governments want a monopoly so they would repress the knowledge and use of such machines and declare them illegal. I would keep my mouth shut about Mr. Mystic and his machine.

Chapter 13

I drove to meet Mrs. MacDougall at her club. The uniformed and very polite attendant at the gate immediately brightened when I mentioned I was Mrs. MacDougall's guest. The maître de at the restaurant informed me in slightly accented English that Mrs. MacDougall was waiting for me and he would happily escort me to her table.

"Good morning Mr. Chandler. Thank you for joining me." She stuck out her hand but didn't rise. She was 85 years old and could remain sitting if she wanted.

I graciously thanked her and said, "I appreciate your invitation for lunch at this magnificent club."

Mrs. MacDougall was drinking a glass of red wine, expensive I'm certain, and asked if I wanted one. I accepted and moments later a glass practically materialized on my right. She raised her half empty glass and said, "To those silver dollars my father loved so much."

We sipped wine and I realized how heavenly it tasted. I usually drink beer, but this contained a different universe of flavors, as unusual as Mr. Mystic and his exceeding strange world. I appreciated it knowing there was no way I could afford this country club, the lavish attention shown her, or even the wine.

Menus appeared and we examined them. She pointed out several unfamiliar items and assured me they were incredibly tasty. Why not?

We ordered and she explained that her father had been a charter member of this club and that she loved sitting in the afternoon sun in one of their solariums. I could only dream, but for today, I lived in her world. Eventually she asked me about my investigation and my detective work regarding Doctor Silver Cartwheel.

"Mrs. MacDougall, it has been different and interesting. The short version is that, yes indeed, Doctor Silver Cartwheel was poisoned by government spending, central banks, greed, and politicians. I can give you the long version if you have time."

She declined the long version but I knew she would want it later. We discussed the slimy politicians and bankers who killed off financial integrity and an important part of American history." She raised her glass and toasted, "What goes around, comes around, and I know they will get what they deserve."

She smiled again and said, "But of course it will all work out in due time. It always does." Our food arrived, she ordered more wine, and we ceased all discussion about business, silver, bankers and politicians.

The food was fabulous, complemented by the wine, and of course I liked and respected Mrs. MacDougall. The restaurant was decorated with conservative elegance, the staff were well trained and somehow materialized precisely when we needed them and otherwise were invisible. I felt almost as overwhelmed as when I watched the silver miners in 1870's Colorado on the remote viewing machine. This was a different world that Mrs. MacDougall had graciously allowed me to visit. I felt honored to experience it.

Mrs. MacDougall was a charming hostess and brought me to tears of laughter and occasional sadness with her stories from years ago. She had the knack for telling a story, making me believe it, and I practically begged for more.

But good things must end and she eventually indicated that our lunch meeting had run its course. Finally she looked directly at me and her mood changed to utter seriousness. "Mr. Chandler, I own a substantial quantity of silver bars and coins. You probably guessed as much. I don't have much time left and I want to make certain I do the right thing with that silver. I can give it to children, grandchildren, and great grandchildren, I can sell it, and I have a few other options. I want you to give me your best estimate of what it will be worth in five years."

I must have looked dumbfounded as she laughed and said, "Yes, I know, you are a detective, not a specialist in the silver market. Yes, I know, you can't predict the future, and you don't have a crystal ball. But I want you to do your best at predicting future prices and tell me what you think. Can you do that for an old lady who doesn't have much time left?"

What could I say? This old lady was a lot more intelligent than me, probably understood the world far better than I did, and she certainly had more wealth than me. I guessed her net worth was over a hundred million dollars. And she had asked me to predict prices and pretended to have naïve faith that I could do it.

"Mrs. MacDougall, I will do my best. That is all I can guarantee." I tried to sound humble and sincere, not scared.

"Mr. Chandler, I'm sure you will. Now if you would help me out of this seat, I need to visit the lady's room. I'll hear from you when you are ready, and I am anxious for your thoughts on the future price of silver."

I helped her up, escorted her to the ladies room, used the men's room, and left her wonderful club.

All the way back to my office I alternated between appreciation for the wine, the meal, and Mrs. MacDougall, and wondering what to do next.

Chapter 14

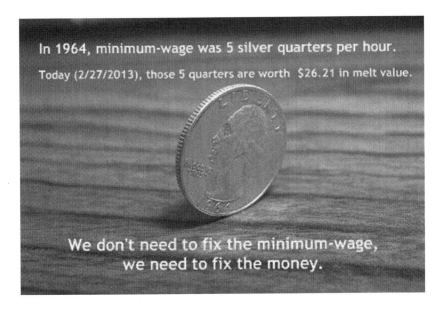

In 1964, minimum-wage was 5 silver quarters per hour.

Today (2/27/2013), those 5 quarters are worth $26.21 in melt value.

We don't need to fix the minimum-wage, we need to fix the money.

Hilda looked up from whatever she was doing and asked brightly, "How was lunch with Mrs. MacDougall?"

"We had wonderful food, very expensive wine, and she is a charmer. I hate to think what the meal and that club cost her but she is obviously wealthy. Every time I talk to her my mental estimate of her net worth goes up."

"I don't suppose you remember the wine and the vintage."

"No, but it was the best I've ever tasted."

"Was she happy with what you told her?"

"Yes, and she even asked me to make a projection for silver prices five years in the future. Now how am I going to do that?"

Hilda grinned mischievously and said, "Guess."

"I've got to do better than that. Think on it. I need all the help I can get."

Back in my office I reviewed my notes on silver, thought more about how to estimate future prices, and gave up. I called Mr. Mystic and asked if I could return for another consultation the next morning.

"Certainly, you are always welcome here. Come by around 9 am." Mr. Mystic was sincere and friendly as always.

Since I was temporarily stuck on future silver prices I worked on the Morrison problem, reread Hilda's report, and decided it was a problem that I would address one piece at a time. I had the names, addresses and pictures of his six important executives. I figured I would start with them, wander by his office building, talk to people, and not arouse suspicions. I switched to blue-collar clothes and drove to his offices for a reconnaissance mission.

I located the office in what is often called the high-rent district. Office buildings were tall and impressive, people on the street were well dressed, and everything looked expensive. I bet myself that a basic well drink would be at least ten bucks in one of the fancy lounges that seemed overly common. Many of the buildings were named after the banks that probably owned them. I assumed a large number of attorneys, accountants, and brokers worked in those buildings, and I saw many restaurants in the area catering to the lunch and dinner crowd.

I was out of place as Zach Chandler, private detective, and really out of place as Zach Child, repairman. I grabbed a battered toolbox out of the trunk to complement my blue-collar clothes and entered the building where Morrison had his offices. The directory displayed an impressive list of important sounding companies, several large law firms, financial planners, two brokerage firms, and others that I forgot immediately. Mr. Morrison's office was on the 12th floor. I looked for other listings on the 12th floor and saw that he had few neighbors.

The man behind the desk in the lobby gave me a hard look which I ignored, and I took the elevator to the 12th floor. After thirty minutes wandering around, snooping, and offering two explanations to suspicious secretaries, I had learned little. I took the elevator to the 7th floor and looked around, saw nothing but expensive office fronts and well-dressed receptionists and hustled out before someone called building security.

I left the building, ignored the man behind the desk in the lobby, and politely opened the door for a twenty-something kid bringing in a small cart of snacks and drinks. He mumbled thanks and I left the building. A van was parked in a loading zone with its flashers on. I read "Horne Office Catering" on the van and assumed I had met the driver.

I drove home and replayed a classic Bobby Fischer chess game since the Rangers were travelling tonight.

Chapter 15

The next morning I called Hilda, told her I was going to Mystic Coins and that I would be back that afternoon. She probably knew that already but didn't indicate such.

Mr. Mystic warmly welcomed me as I entered his store and directed me to his office. After we were comfortably seated he asked, "And what can I do for you today?"

Ordinarily I would have been hesitant to talk about predicting the future, but Mr. Mystic had already shown me things that happened in the past, so why not five years into the future. "I want to impose on your hospitality and knowledge again. I spoke with my client about silver dollars, and she wants more information. In fact, she wants something quite difficult. She wants a prediction for silver prices five years in the future." I still had not told him my client was Mrs. MacDougall but he certainly knew and that was why he gave me special consideration.

Mr. Mystic smiled and said, "That is the sixty-four trillion dollar question that everyone wants answered. I wish you luck."

Hmmm. He was not helpful like I had hoped. "Mr. Mystic, you gave me a very impressive history lesson with the help of your remote viewing machine. I was hoping you could run the machine in the opposite direction and show me the future. Specifically, what will silver prices be in several years, and just to satisfy my curiosity, which corrupt politician will we elect in 2016?"

Apparently he saw no humor in the 2016 election question and he wasn't happy about me asking to peek into the future.

"Mr. Chandler, you do not understand. The future is uncertain, unlike the past. What would happen if someone went bonkers in a missile silo and launched an ICBM toward Russia or toward the United States? The future would be very different if that event did, or did not happen."

He waited for me to show that I understood. "But aren't there high probability events that are likely to occur and wouldn't your machine see those events, even if the rest were fuzzy and unclear?"

He tried to explain. "There are several issues. The machine is amazing at what it can show in the past, but the future is difficult to predict because there are many possible threads. Suppose we look forward to the election in 2016 and watch the victory speeches to see who wins the presidential race. If we look forward today we might see that candidate X will be elected. Tomorrow the machine might show candidate X narrowly losing."

He smiled as he tried to explain. "The machine can see several threads but which one will actually occur is not yet certain. If the machine saw one outcome 99 times and a different outcome once I would conclude that the majority outcome was likely, but that is all we can know."

"Besides, the machine uses tremendous energy going forward and the "Nothing Box" has to be given time to recharge. Further, the images become very fuzzy and unclear after about five years and basically useless after about ten years. Do you see the problem?"

"I am beginning to see the problem, but can we try anyway?"

"Mr. Chandler, I will do this for you, but on my terms only. We will get three views of the future five years from now. We will do one view per day, and will look at downtown Dallas, Wall Street, and the financial markets. Each view will be brief so we don't overtax the Nothing Box, and we will discuss only on the third day after all three views are complete. I think you will see the difficulty in what you ask after these three viewings."

He hesitated, looked intently at me, and I felt another tingle run up my spine. He had a special presence. "I agree, and I thank you. Can we begin today?"

"Come this way to the Archive room."

After I was comfortably seated he fiddled with the controls and announced, "Remember, I told you it will be blurry and this is only one possible future."

"I remember." I leaned forward in anticipation.

"This is version one for middle 2020, five years out. I'm showing you downtown Dallas at high noon on a Friday."

What I saw was somewhat blurry. I could see traffic and people walking on the streets and at first glance it looked about the same as 2015, except there were more small cars and bicycles on the streets. We watched cars, pedestrians, many city streets, and buildings for several minutes. Mr. Mystic shifted the scene to Wall Street and I read headlines on a very large screen in a financial building. I learned that the Federal Reserve had expanded their money printing games to over a trillion dollars each quarter, and that the stock market was higher. The Dow flashed across the screen at 26,000 and change but it might have been 36,000. I saw the price of silver and read either $68 or $88 per ounce. The image was so unclear that I could not tell a "6" from an "8." I saw a headline about sending more soldiers to fight in some country but could not make out what country or why.

The screen went blank and Mr. Mystic said, "That's all for today. The "Nothing Box" is down to 20% power and needs to recharge. Come back tomorrow at 9 am and do not think about what you have seen until we are finished with all three viewings and we have discussed them."

I thanked him and left but I couldn't ignore what the remote viewing screen had shown me. I thought about it all the way back to the office.

Hilda greeted me with, "You don't look so good. Can I get you a cup of coffee?"

Apparently I had been obsessing over version one. "Yes, please."

I needed to work on the Morrison case to get my mind off the future.

Chapter 16

I slept poorly because I worried about what day two at Mystic Coins would show me. Maybe knowing the future was a bad idea.

I started with a heavy breakfast that included eggs, sausage, and fried potatoes. The waitress refilled my coffee cup at least three times. By the time I arrived at Mystic Coins I was ready, or so I thought.

We entered the Archive Room and he fired up the remote viewing machine, cautioned me not to obsess over anything I saw, and put us into downtown Dallas, as before. This viewing was much different from the Dallas I had expected. I saw few people and cars on the streets and those streets were practically deserted. Some of the large office buildings were boarded up with plywood as if Dallas were expecting a hurricane. The whole scene was bleak, depressing and sad.

The screen blanked out and then refocused on Wall Street. I saw armed guards, several burned out buildings, many for sale and for lease signs, and few people on the streets. A screen in a financial building that was still open for business displayed headlines and market prices. The Dow Index was about 7000, most of the headlines were about depressed economic conditions, unemployment, emergency government programs, extra police forces, riots, food shortages, and other depressing circumstances. I think the price of silver was about $60 but I couldn't be certain. Everything I saw was depressed and dark. A special announcement interrupted the headlines and the commentator cut to a video feed from the White House and the President of the United States. She made an announcement, which I could barely hear, that had something to do with a retaliatory strike against another country, maybe Russia. Apparently there was depression and war in this future. I liked it less than what I had seen yesterday.

The screen went blank and Mr. Mystic cautioned me about believing what I had seen. He told me to come again the next morning.

Hilda took one look at me and said, "Boss, do you need to go home?" I told her no and retreated to my office and the morning newspaper. The ugly financial, social, and political headlines were positively benign compared to what I had seen in version two of the year 2020. I read more and returned to the world of 2015, which appeared better and better.

Eventually I felt up to working on the Morrison case, which had developed several interesting twists. I was gone the rest of the day.

I slept better that night but woke with a feeling of dread. I started with another heavy breakfast and lots of coffee. The waitress looked at me with pity. I think she thought I was facing a prison sentence or an IRS audit based on how I looked and how she treated me.

I drove to Mystic Coins to see another possible future scenario. I had serious doubts about the wisdom of trying to look into the future. It was hazardous to my mental health.

We entered the Archive Room on the 3rd day and I sat down with no expectation but a ton of worry and concern.

Mr. Mystic said, "You see that knowing the future is not always a good thing. Frankly you don't look well. I told you not to think about what you have seen but it looks like you couldn't help yourself."

He was kind and did not say, "It serves you right, or be careful what you ask for, you might get it." I sat and waited.

The screen lit up and we saw Dallas again. This version looked similar to day one, a moderate amount of activity, cars and people moved about, and life looked more normal. But I noticed many homeless people and I saw rows of cardboard boxes arranged on sidewalks where people were sleeping. I saw long lines of people waiting to get a paper plate of food. I also saw a queue of people wanting to gas up their tiny cars. I had a very bad feeling about what I would see in New York.

The viewer shifted to Wall Street where I saw considerable activity along with many homeless and a number of police units patrolling the streets. The headlines scrolling across the large screen indicated that the Dow had risen over 200,000, the minimum wage had been raised to $175 per hour, and people were protesting recent increases in the price of coffee at Starbucks. Apparently a Grande was currently selling for $79 and likely to increase to $99 next month. Silver was priced at $1,500 I think, but it might have been $1,800. Hyperinflation had come to the United States and I saw nothing to recommend it. The screen showed a video clip of jet fighters attacking and destroying a city but I missed whose jets and what city. The screen went blank and frankly, I was relieved.

"Now do you see why I was reluctant to show you future possibilities?"

I shook myself to come back to the present and said, "Yes, I get it now."

"So, Mr. Chandler, what did you make of each of those possible futures?" He sounded sad, not smug, like he was concerned that I would over-react to what I had seen. Based on how I felt, looked, and had been sleeping, he had good reason to worry.

I thought about the three views, what they indicated, and realized I had not learned what I had expected. "I suppose those three possible futures can be described as more of the same, depression, and hyperinflation. It seemed that higher silver prices, more human misery, war, and social chaos were common elements. The first day was the best, but all three looked like we have difficult times ahead."

"And if you saw a fourth day, it might show a much better world, happier people, fewer homeless, more honest politicians, and less war. We don't know what will happen and that's why we worry and desire clear answers about something which can never be precise."

"I understand better now. We shouldn't worry about the future, we live each day, work to improve our lives, plan as best we can, and move on. But I have to say, all three futures looked ugly and difficult."

"If you had looked into the future on January 1, 2000 would you have been shocked seeing the damage from the 9-11 attack, the political reaction it caused, the invasion of Iraq, and the financial crisis of 2008?" He paused, handed me a cup of coffee, and continued, "But we are still here. Markets have recovered, crude oil and silver prices are much higher, we live in a more dangerous and depressing world, but life goes on. No matter what happens there are certain things you can plan on. How they affect everything else and your attitude determine the future you will live in."

I shook my head in agreement and asked, "So if we can't see the future, what can we plan on?"

He ticked off items on his fingers. "More debt and more government spending. Politics, corruption, and stupidity. Higher prices, market booms and busts, and war. Asking people to give up political favors, spending, debt, and war is like asking 20 year old young adults to give up sex. It will not happen except in rare circumstances. Maybe the world continues down the same silly path it is on, or maybe we crash into a depression, or maybe we go crazy printing money and become Zimbabwe on the Potomac. Probably we should expect all three to one degree or another. In fact, some thinkers believe that excess spending and massive debt will force the global economy into a depression and the central bankers of the world will fight that depression with massive money printing and thereby create hyperinflation. Frankly, that is what I expect but I don't have a PhD in economics and therefore my opinion doesn't count."

I think he was being sarcastic about the PhD economists. Otherwise I believed his interpretation of what we could plan on and I wanted to forget the three futures that I had seen.

We chatted for another hour but it was only to add perspective to what we had seen for the year 2020. I still did not know the future or what the price of silver would be, but it was clear to me that silver prices would be higher, probably far higher, and definitely not lower.

"Thank you for your time, your consideration, and the visions of the future. I will respect your confidence." I left and drove back to the office.

Chapter 17

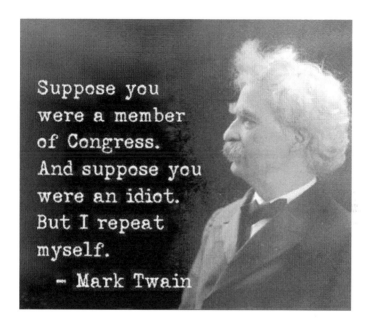

Suppose you were a member of Congress. And suppose you were an idiot. But I repeat myself.

— Mark Twain

Hilda looked at me when I walked into the office, sighed, and said, "Boss, I think this case is getting to you. I haven't seen you looking this badly in years."

I had been thinking about other options for predicting silver prices and so I was ready. "Bingo. I have been sleeping poorly, wanting to drink again, and I'm ready for a new approach. What I need from you are the titles of books, magazines, and the names of analysis that discuss future silver prices. Skip everything from Nobel Prize winners, central bankers, and PhD economists. Mrs. MacDougall is skeptical of them and I'll take her word for it."

Hilda smiled and said, "Coming up. Good to see you back in the land of the living. You looked positively wretched yesterday."

I could always depend upon Hilda for the truth, but not compliments. I figured it would take her a day or two for her research and that gave me time to explore another idea I had about the Morrison case. I trusted that he had done everything possible investigating phone calls, wireless transmissions, the internet, and more that I didn't understand. He had found nothing so that indicated the leak was either very sophisticated and had not yet been found, or it was very simple in an old fashioned sense. I was good with old fashioned sleuthing and I wanted to observe the office building all afternoon and make notes. Sometimes I get a tingle in the back of my neck that alerts me to something important that appears ordinary.

I went looking for something that would give me a tingle.

I spent four hours watching, changing positions, walking in and out of the building, chatting up people, and … no tingle.

The Rangers lost that night by 9 to 1 or worse. I gave up in the 7th inning and replayed another Bobby Fischer chess match when he was only 17. Pure genius! It takes both geniuses like Fischer and throw-backs like me to make the world. I knew my talents and wasn't worried that I would never play chess like Fischer.

Chapter 18

The next day Hilda gave me books, several magazines, and a long list of people regarding silver. She called a couple of them technicians or technical analysts. She told me four of them were morons and that a couple others were so unusual that even if they did make sense, I would not believe them. Hilda pointed out three that she thought I should explore. That meant reading articles and a couple of books. I read the titles and got a headache.

I told her I was going to the library but I really intended to get a cup of overpriced coffee at my favorite diner and think about what I wanted, what was important, and how to approach the subject.

Hilda responded with, "Don't drink too much coffee. It's hard on your adrenals."

How did she know I was going to the diner?

After my coffee I drove to the library, found my favorite librarian, gave her three writers and waited. Soon she brought me a stack of books, some printed articles, and several technical magazines I had never seen before.

Several hours later I realized that these analysts who discussed future silver prices were convincing but they often disagreed. I did not know what or who to believe and felt like the blind man asked to describe an elephant.

I reviewed my notes and decided to drive by the Morrison offices.

I found a patch of shade, parked, fed the meter and watched, and watched, and watched. It was boring work and I had accomplished absolutely nothing. I noticed a truck stop in the loading zone in front of the building. Soon the driver walked to the front door holding a bouquet of flowers. Someone was either apologizing or anxious to get into someone's good graces. I approved.

Fifteen minutes later a UPS truck stopped and the driver took a hand truck full of parcels into the building. He left the building ten minutes later with one package that he had picked up inside.

Half an hour later I saw the Horne Office Catering truck ease to a stop in the loading zone and a few minutes later the driver wheeled a cart filled with snacks, drinks, and coffee into the building. I needed a cup of coffee and almost wandered over to chat with him but decided against it.

He was inside for 20 to 30 minutes. When he returned his snack cart was nearly empty. My neck tingled. I thought about the fact that he is there every day, collects cash from various people, and is anonymous. Nobody would suspect him. I grabbed my camera with the long lens and took photos of the truck, the license plate and the driver. I followed him and noted all his subsequent stops.

The more I followed him the more I was certain something about this route was important. Three hours later I had a list of addresses and office building names where he stopped. I bet myself that he had a regular route and, like clockwork, he showed up every day at about the same time.

About 4:30 he was done and drove back to his warehouse. My tingle disappeared and I went home.

The next morning I wanted to tackle the silver issue but I wasn't ready to wade through a bunch of numbers, statistics, and graphs that made little sense. I decided to work on the Morrison case.

I started with a phone book and the names of the office buildings on the Horne route. I gave my notes to Hilda, asked her to organize them, make them legible, and I asked her to research any names I had missed. I also asked her to highlight the financial firms that might be interested in Morrison business. With that project moving forward I decided to tackle the silver issue.

I went over my notes, tried to make sense of the charts and analysis, and accomplished little. Terms like stochastics, relative strength, open interest, mining supply, EBITDA, MACD, oscillators, log-scale charts, all-in costs, support and resistance, triangle patterns, time cycles, Fibonacci retracement levels, and a hundred others just did not register with me. I needed help.

I thought about talking to one of the analysts recommended by Hilda but that did not appeal to me. I considered another coin store but I assumed they would just tell me silver was going to the moon and that I should buy from them today.

I sipped cold coffee for a moment and received an inspiration. I trusted Mr. Mystic and Mrs. MacDougall. I would find an analyst who shared their ideas and skip the PhD's and Nobel Prize winners. I noted on my yellow pad:

1. The governments of the world will create more debt and continue spending as long as they can.
2. Politics, corruption, lies, and stupidity are everywhere and will persist. Expect more in the upcoming years.
3. Expect much higher prices for the stuff we need, like food and energy, because all central banks were printing currencies and devaluing the existing currency in the system.
4. Expect market booms and busts, since there always have been booms and busts. Expect the booms and busts to become more intense since the markets have been distorted and manipulated by government spending and central bank interventions.
5. Expect more war. Politicians like war because it pays well, either in graft, conquered land, stolen oil, confiscated gold, or captured markets.
6. The Chinese, Russian, and Indian people and their central banks were accumulating gold and silver with good reason. After handling gold and silver coins I believed that gold and silver were far more real and enduring than digital or paper dollars, euros, and yen. Apparently the Chinese, Russians, and Indians agreed and trusted the metal more than debt based paper.
7. The global financial system would continue down the same silly path until it crashed into a depression, or maybe a crazy money printing hyperinflation, or possibly both.
8. Paper money only survives a few decades before a government or central bank destroys it by creating too much, unless it is backed by something real like gold. The global financial system is currently in trouble but few are admitting the obvious.
9. I remembered Mr. Mystic talking about Zimbabwe on the Potomac. It was a grim thought but he might be correct.

I needed an analyst who accepted this view of the financial world. I went back to books and magazine articles searching for analysts who would agree with the points I had written on my yellow pad. It turned out that many silver analysts saw the world in the same terms as Mr. Mystic and many were skeptical regarding the durability of the existing system. I continued reading and making notes, which increased my interest in the silver story.

I tried to consolidate their ideas, analysis, and graphs into simple terms that would appeal to Mr. Mystic and Mrs. MacDougall. I found some analysis and models that seemed important. Many of these analysts were highly intelligent but skeptical of current thinking in the world of PhD economists. Since I agreed with the skeptics, I continued.

The first chart was population adjusted national debt from 1971 extended out to 2025. I saw no good reason for national debt to suddenly contract given our current batch of corrupt borrow and spend politicians. Hence I figured this chart was sensible. In fact, it was probably conservative as I assumed more spending and more war, not less, were on the horizon.

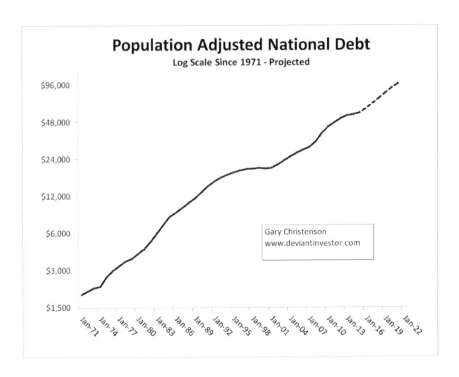

Population Adjusted National Debt

Log Scale Since 1971 - Projected

Gary Christenson
www.deviantinvestor.com

The next chart was the same population adjusted national debt but shown along with annual silver prices, heavily smoothed with moving averages. After smoothing the erratic silver prices it was easy to see that both lines were increasing exponentially more or less together. I had read that silver supply was increasing slowly or not at all, and some analysts expected supply to flat line in a few years. Further, industrial demand and investment demand seemed to be increasing far more rapidly than mining supply. I saw no reason to believe that silver prices would stay low when debt and demand were accelerating higher.

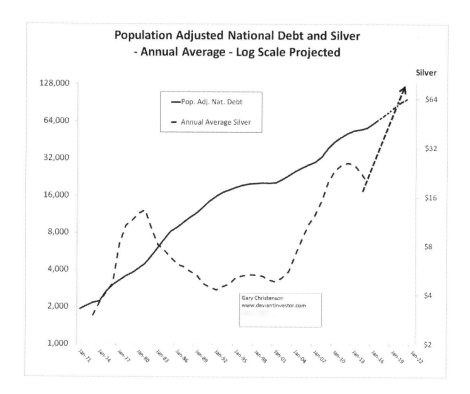

The next chart showed the silver to gold ratio chart back to 1985. That chart was difficult to understand but the analysts concluded:

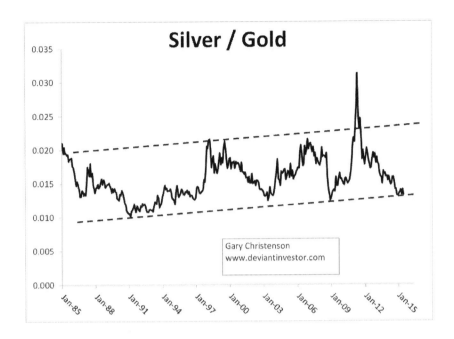

- Silver and gold prices moved higher and lower together.
- When the ratio was low, silver prices were weak and when the ratio was high, silver prices were high.
- Another way of describing the ratio was to say that silver rose more rapidly and fell harder than gold, so the ratio went to extremes.
- The ratio was historically low in 2015. Hence silver prices were too low, based on 30 years of history, and were likely to substantially increase in the coming years.

The next chart showed the ratio of silver to S&P 500 Index for 30 years, starting after the massive bubble in silver prices that ended in 1980. The S&P 500 Index, like silver prices, increased erratically but exponentially over time. This ratio also showed that silver prices were currently low compared to the S&P 500 Index, which suggested that silver prices were likely to rise, and possibly the S&P 500 Index would fall. Some analysts were calling for a stock market crash but others pointed out that the government and the central banks wanted the S&P 500 Index and other stock markets to remain high, so they were confident the stock market would correct somewhat but not crash. I had my doubts about the ability of the government to prevent crashes, but I was a private detective, not a stock analyst.

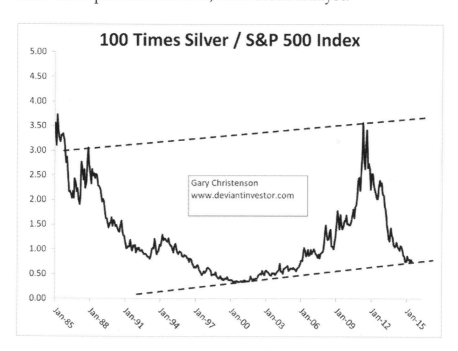

The next chart showed the S&P 500 Index since 1985 added to 100 times the price of silver, which made them about equal in weight. This chart clearly showed that the sum of the two moved upward exponentially, probably because so much money was printed into circulation every decade and it had to go into prices somewhere. When silver was strong the S&P was often weak and vice versa, but on average the sum of the two climbed higher.

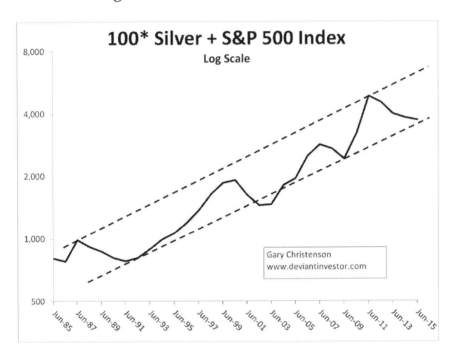

I looked at what one analyst had written about the ratio and sum of silver and the S&P. He noted that the ratio showed that silver was currently low compared to the S&P and had been for several years. But assuming that politicians kept spending and debt increased as usual, the sum would continue increasing. He showed the high end of the chart for 2020 at about 8,000 and suggested that if silver rallied in the next five years and if the S&P either corrected or crashed and recovered, then silver prices might average $60 or so in 2020. The analyst suggested a range of prices from $40 to over $100, and strongly suggested that more money printing, out of control debt, wars, increased industrial and investment demand, and flat or slowly increasing supply should push silver to the high end of the range or higher.

I liked his thinking and assumed that Mrs. MacDougall would approve. Picking a range from his analysis suggested that $75 - $100 was a reasonable target for silver in 2020, and much higher if conditions became crazy with hyperinflation, and maybe somewhat less if the world descended into another deflationary depression.

I thought Mr. Mystic would approve.

Another analyst had another model for prices. He used a similar approach based on debt, which he thought was practically guaranteed to increase, along with the price for crude oil and the S&P 500 Index. He showed the price of silver and crude oil beside each other and noted that they often did not move together when viewed year by year, but in the long term they moved up, just like the national debt and the stock market. Mr. Mystic had shown this slide to me.

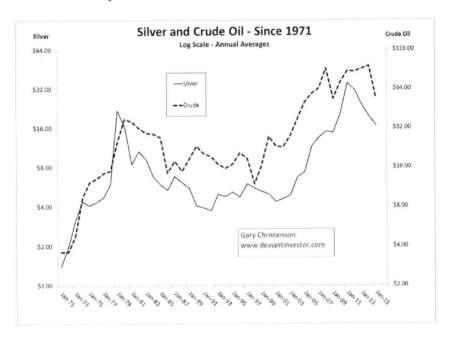

He also noted, like the other analyst, that silver and the S&P 500 Index moved in opposite directions in the short term, but that in the long term they both moved up. This analyst described it as changing investor preference between commodities and financial assets. When investors wanted financial assets, such as between 1980 and 2000, the stock market went up strongly and commodities went down on average. The reverse had been true from 2001 to 2011, but then the stock market took off again in 2011 while commodities corrected or crashed.

This analyst said he had constructed a model based on the exponential increases in national debt, adjusted higher by the price of crude oil and lower by the value of the S&P 500 Index. He claimed the model was a valuation model, not a timing model, and that it accurately portrayed the average price of silver going back over a century. He included this graph of the smoothed annual price of silver and the values calculated by his model. The statistical correlation between the actual smoothed price of silver with the calculated price was better than 0.95. The lines looked similar to me but I was skeptical whether or not the model would work five or ten years into the future. This was especially true after the vision of three different futures that I had seen at Mr. Mystic's office. They still haunted me but I refused to dwell on them.

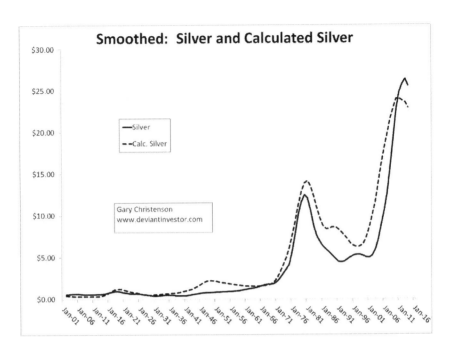

Smoothed: Silver and Calculated Silver

Gary Christenson
www.deviantinvestor.com

I read further to see what he had to say about the price of silver in the next five to ten years. He noted that predicting the price of the S&P 500 Index was difficult since he thought the influence of government and central bank buying would distort prices higher, but he assumed that if the S&P continued up strongly after a correction, the national debt would probably accelerate even more rapidly and the model would compensate for those two variables. He produced this graph of projected average values for silver.

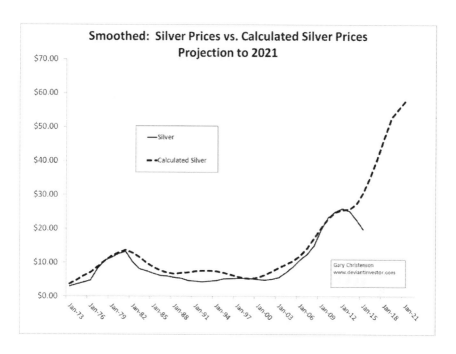

Smoothed: Silver Prices vs. Calculated Silver Prices Projection to 2021

I liked the idea but remembered that even the remote viewer could not accurately show what would happen, so I interpreted his model as a reasonable valuation but not a prediction for prices. Regardless, his model showed $75 as a reasonable average silver price for 2020. He also noted that while $75 might be a reasonable valuation, actual prices could temporarily spike far higher or lower, like $50 to $150, and that was only if the monetary geniuses in charge did not create a hyperinflationary Zimbabwe on the Potomac scenario.

I found another model based on Fibonacci retracements, Elliott Waves, and other timing and ratios I did not understand. The final prediction for silver in five to ten years was much higher, well into three digits.

I also read a few articles from the analysts that Hilda had called morons. I thought they sounded intelligent but I could not see their rationale for silver prices under $10 when our government seemed hell-bent on pumping dollars into every financial nook and cranny to prop up an increasingly unstable paper money system. I visualized a house of cards and how easily it could crash. But the PhD's were in charge and I was only a detective, and I hoped they had learned something from the last several crashes.

Most of the analysts discussed the possibility of financial accidents and systemic crashes, and in those cases they admitted these models might be way off. For instance, if the world financial system crashed like it did in the 1930's depression and real estate and stock prices went into the toilet, perhaps silver prices would be weak, but others thought a depression would drive stocks and real estate far lower, but silver much higher. There was often no consensus.

Even worse was the possibility of Zimbabwe on the Potomac – hyperinflation. If the government printed money like other governments in hyperinflations, then all bets were off. I had not realized that hyperinflations had been common in the 20th century. I had heard about the German hyperinflation in the early 1920's but according to these writers, there had been a number of hyperinflations since the year 1900. One person noted that Argentina had lopped off 9 or maybe 10 zeros from their money over the past 40 years. That sounded like fiscal mismanagement but apparently mismanagement and inflation were the norm in Argentina. I decided that it is impossible to predict how bad the consequences will be when governments and central banks start down the money printing path propelled by greed, politics, desperation, ignorance and stupidity.

I pondered that thought for a moment and realized that the United States had been printing money like never before. Yes, the money supply had increased since 1913 and especially since 1971 when Nixon severed the link between the dollar and gold, but the Federal Reserve had gone into financially uncharted territory with Quantitative Easing since the 2008 financial crisis. How different were we from Argentina and Zimbabwe?

Clearly there were many differences and one of them was that the United States had the reserve currency used globally. About then my headache came back and I realized I was in way over my head trying to understand global economics, money printing, hyperinflations and deflations. I went back to basics and told myself that the government and politicians will continue spending, central banks will print currencies, debt and spending are clearly out of control, and something bad is likely to happen. Maybe hyperinflation was not only possible, but likely. Politicians don't suddenly become ethical, bankers don't become less greedy, human nature does not change, and therefore silver was going much higher. I had no way to know how crazy the spending, debt, and money printing would become, so there was no way to know how much higher silver prices would climb.

I concluded that these analysts were probably correct in stating that silver prices would move much higher. I asked myself what a Nobel Prize winning economist would say about silver and decided I didn't know and didn't care. But I knew what I believed. Silver was safer and more reliable than digital and paper money, and it would be priced far higher in upcoming years. The remote viewing machine had shown that if the government and central bankers created hyperinflation, silver would be priced at some insanely high price. But if the world crashed into another great depression, as the remote viewer had also shown as a possibility, even then silver would probably be worth much more than paper money. Also, I remembered that many banks went broke in the depression and I assumed it would be worse this time. That was another reason why the central banks of the world would print money until they had lost all credibility – they would take care of themselves and their wealthy owners at the expense of the middle class and the poor.

I was done for the day. My head hurt and I left the office. Even Hilda was gone and she usually stayed longer than me.

The Rangers had a no-hitter going into the 9th inning when the Ranger pitcher served up a fast ball that got away from him. It hung right over the plate and the batter smacked it into right-center for a solo home run. Things can change quickly. I went to bed and dreamed about debt monsters that devoured cities and crushed skyscrapers.

Chapter 19

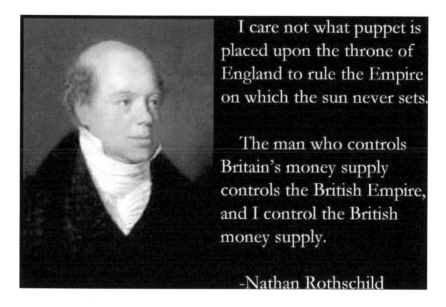

I care not what puppet is placed upon the throne of England to rule the Empire on which the sun never sets.

The man who controls Britain's money supply controls the British Empire, and I control the British money supply.

-Nathan Rothschild

When I walked into the office Hilda handed me a pile of papers with the Morrison information organized by building, time of delivery, and on a separate sheet, by businesses potentially associated with Morrison. As usual, Hilda had created a masterpiece.

I sat down and studied it for an hour, thought about possibilities, imagined very sneaky and intelligent financial people trying to communicate discretely, carefully, and reliably. I tried to think like a CIA spy shadowing a Russian agent. I decided that simple was better, no direct contact was essential, and a dead drop would work but a personal delivery man was easier, quicker, safer and probably more consistent with the thinking of a financial analyst who was betraying his boss by divulging inside information.

I narrowed down the list of possible competitors to two likely candidates with three more possibilities. Now was the time for snooping and legwork. I checked the schedule and realized I had three hours to work on the silver case before I had to be on duty watching the Horne truck.

The silver case had become more interesting every day. I studied my notes, poured over the graphs again, and lost myself in the study of silver for over two hours. I checked my watch, put the silver papers away and drove to follow the Horne delivery truck.

I followed the driver, entered the buildings of the five identified businesses, stayed out of sight from the driver, and watched. He was doing his job, was pleasant to everyone, earned good tips, and had personal contact with several hundred people each day. He was paid in cash, stuffed the bills in a small bag, and distributed coffee, soda, energy drinks, chips, and other packaged food to people in need of an afternoon pick-me-up or a food break.

He had a good business but I couldn't watch it for days until the next hot deal was leaked. I needed to accelerate the time table and observe on the day that Morrison discussed the deal with his staff. I asked a receptionist if there was a payphone in the building and called Mr. Morrison. We agreed that he would announce the possibility of a deal the next Tuesday, and I would be waiting.

I planned to replay another Bobby Fischer chess game that night, but instead I reviewed all the silver information. It was a compelling story. I reviewed what I had learned and seen at Mystic Coins, and decided there were missing pieces of information but I had enough to give a good presentation to Mrs. MacDougall.

I checked the Ranger game but lost interest after two batters grounded out and they were behind by four runs.

Chapter 20

I organized the silver story as best I could, added graphs and information from several analysts, and handed it to Hilda to improve. She would tweak it here and there, improve the analysis, and make it presentable.

I went to the library and read about gold because silver and gold were real money, intimately connected, and precious metals. Since today was Friday I had four days before the Morrison leak of the next hot deal. After several hours learning about gold, I decided I needed to know more about the driver of the Horne Catering business. I knew his last stop and waited for him late that afternoon.

I followed him home, drove by his house, and learned little.

On Monday morning I asked Hilda to research him, added her comments to what I had observed, and decided that George Blair was a decent person, 22 years old, living with his mother in a tiny house in a nothing special suburb of Dallas, and that he and she were getting by. He had nothing in his background that aroused my interest and he seemed to be a steady and reliable employee.

Hilda handed me the silver report for Mrs. MacDougall and told me, "Good job boss. I think your silver analysis was excellent. I haven't mentioned it before, but my husband and I are stackers. We collect silver coins and bars that we view as retirement insurance in case the whole financial system goes bonkers. I think your estimate of $75 to $100 as an average price for silver in the year 2020 is too low, but I can't fault the reasoning of those analysts."

Hilda surprises me often. I just sat there for a moment and thought, "Who knew Hilda was into silver?"

Instead I said, "Thanks. What do you think Mrs. MacDougall will say?"

"She will tell you that silver has been crushed for the past four years by the banking and political interests who need to support a failing dollar. Consequently, when silver finally does adjust to a more realistic price, it will rally too far and too fast and probably blow through $100 per ounce." She smiled at me cynically and continued, "And that is because she is immensely critical of the money printing scoundrels who infest central banks."

Like I said, Hilda surprises me. "Can I quote you as a reliable and informed source who wishes to remain off the record?"

"Boss, be serious. That lady is smarter than both of us and she knows what is happening in the world of silver, gold, and paper money. I think she just wanted another interpretation from someone who had no preconceived notions on the subject."

"Hmmm. So I'll call and ask her if she wants to come in or if I should meet her somewhere."

"Yes, but she'll want to meet you somewhere."

I called and Hilda was correct. I arranged to meet Mrs. MacDougall on Wednesday at her club.

I had little to do for the rest of the afternoon so I took a walk in the park, watched children play, and tried not to take the craziness of the world seriously.

***

Tuesday was the big day for the Morrison project. He called me at 10 am and told me that all six of his assistants knew the name of the next target. He also said it was plausible but not true, but to the best of his knowledge, the assistants believed it. He told me to do my stuff and bring him an answer.

It wasn't easy, and I was lucky, but I deconstructed the puzzle.

I explained it all to him in my office later that week. "The critical issues were who and how. I watched the driver, a Mr. Blair, after he left your office on Tuesday. He seemed tense and more agitated than usual. When he returned to his truck he took a small piece of paper out of his collection bag and stuck it in his back pocket. I assumed he had been given the paper at his afternoon delivery. I followed him and watched carefully at each of the five targeted businesses. When he reached Gillingham and Stone I got lucky and saw him remove the note from his back pocket, obviously preparing to pass the note. I could not position myself to see who he passed the note to, but it didn't matter."

Morrison's leaned forward and looked intense. I could almost hear him say, "Out with it man, I'm anxious and waiting."

"To cut a long story short I watched him the rest of the day, noticed nothing unusual, followed him home, and had a frank chat with him that night. He wasn't anxious to explain what happened but I strongly encouraged him to talk to me rather than someone more unfriendly. He evaluated his options and explained the process."

I paused for effect, watched Morrison's face and continued. "Every so often one of your employees orders a coffee and offers Mr. Blair a $100 bill in payment. He tells Blair to keep the change, which is the signal. Inside the folded bill is a piece of paper. The note on the paper means nothing to Blair since it is written in code. Blair mentioned that your employee's name is Tony."

Morrison's face initially registered hurt, then anger, and finally sadness. He said, "Go on."

"Blair hands the piece of paper inside a dollar bill in change to another person named Cecil over at Gillingham and Stone, and that is the story. Blair has no clue what is happening or why. He just knows that he collects an extra hundred bucks occasionally and does not ask questions."

Morrison sat quietly and thought for a few moments. "I'll deal with Tony. I would not have guessed it was him. I know Cecil and I will find some way to express my displeasure with him. I will say nothing to Mr. Blair. Perhaps you can strongly encourage him not to engage in these little games and hand him, say five one hundred dollar bills. He takes the money, shuts up, never does it again, and we all forgive and forget. Otherwise I won't be so kind. Make certain he understands."

"I can chat with Mr. Blair and I'm confident he will see the value in what you suggest and in taking a $500 termination fee."

"Mr. Chandler, it has been a pleasure doing business with you. Tally up what I owe you and I'll make good on my promise for that bonus after I confirm that Tony is my problem employee." He rose, shook my hand and left.

I had done a proper job, set a few things right, and felt good about it.

Chapter 21

The next day I drove to Mrs. MacDougall's club for lunch. I was greeted like an old friend. I thought they laid it on a bit thick, but what do I know about managing a classy country club?

Mrs. MacDougall was sipping wine when I was led to her table. She smiled at me and we chatted for a while. I felt like she was an elderly and eccentric aunt, one I respected and liked. We ordered, sipped wine, and finally got to the silver business after lunch, desert, and coffee.

"So who killed Doctor Silver Cartwheel?"

I explained as best I could. "Doctor Silver Cartwheel was poisoned by politicians and bankers. The politicians spent gobs of money they didn't have for many years , borrowed the difference, created inflation, devalued the dollar, and that pushed the price of silver so high the silver in one of those cartwheels was worth more than a dollar, so the government stopped minting them. Naturally the silver dollars disappeared from circulation and people hoarded them."

"Apparently responsibly managing the budget and eliminating the inflation was never considered an option by the politicians. Eventually the bankers talked President Nixon into abandoning the dollar to gold convertibility, and that gave the bankers and politicians free reign to create a huge number of new dollars. They eliminated the possibility of using real money, so now we use that nasty paper stuff you dislike."

She smiled a bit and said, "Don't forget this dreadful plastic money." She removed an American Express card from her purse and looked sadly at it. "Times change and we must adapt, even if we don't want to change. Which reminds me, what will silver be worth in another five years?"

Mrs. MacDougall had a twinkle in her eye. As Hilda had said, she was smarter than both of us. I pretended not to notice and said, "I have my report here." I tapped the report I had laid on the table. "But the bottom line is that, based on my research, the help I received from Mr. Mystic, and the analysis of several bright silver researchers, I think average silver prices will be in the $75 to $100 range in five years. But if our central bank and administration go crazy printing dollars, or we have a financial catastrophe that pushes the country into hyperinflation, silver might sell for $1,000 per ounce. Who can be certain?"

She added, "Actually, the hyperinflation, if it happens, might not be created on Wall Street or in Washington. It might be generated in Europe or Asia and exported to our economy. We don't know what the global politicians or their banker owners have planned. But I'm certain we will increase debt, corruption, the power of the politicians and the influence of the financial community."

We discussed silver for another 15 minutes. Finally she said, "Well, Mr. Chandler, I'm anxious to study your report. Now, about your bill..."

She had that twinkle in her eye again. "You can send me a final bill and I can send you a check. Or, I can take your final bill, divide it by the price of silver that day, and give you a call. If you decide you want silver bars or coins, I will ship them to your office instead of writing you a check."

She paused, saw my blank look, and said, "Think on it. I'll call you after you send me a final bill."

We chatted for another ten minutes and I left. Mrs. MacDougall was an interesting lady.

The Rangers pitched a shutout that night and won 4-0. Maybe they had a chance for the pennant after all.

Chapter 22

A few days later I received a check in the mail from Mr. Morrison. True to his word he had added a bonus of $25,000. That same afternoon Mrs. MacDougall called.

I had sent her a bill for $11,500, which I calculated as about equivalent to 715 ounces of silver.

"So, Mr. Chandler, what have you decided?" She made it sound like I was answering a question on a final exam.

"Mrs. MacDougall, I accept your gracious offer. I calculate that my bill is equal to about 700 ounces of silver. I will be happy with two 100 ounce bars plus 500 silver eagles."

"Mr. Chandler, I'm confident you made an excellent choice. Expect a delivery via Fed Ex in a few days."

She hung up and I sat back and relaxed. I did not want to obsess over the future, but I was certain I would rather own silver than not own silver. I was absolutely certain that I would rather have silver coins than loan my digital dollars to my bank by making a deposit into my checking account.

I also thought that I would give Hilda 100 silver eagles and one bar as a bonus. She was invaluable to me and she stacked silver as insurance against the craziness in our political and financial systems.

It had been a good year so far. I wondered who would walk through the office door with new and interesting business in the next month.

I raised my coffee cup to toast Mrs. MacDougall, Mr. Mystic, and Hilda, and happily stated, "It's a wonderful life because we make it so."

The End.

Acknowledgements

I sincerely thank my wife for support and assistance in writing this book, editing the text, acting as my sounding board, and encouraging me along the way.

Robin Berthier is the imaginative artist who created the art for the front and back covers. I thank him for capturing the essence of the story in his images. You may contact him at www.paperwaves.be.

About the Author

Gary Christenson is the owner and writer for the popular investment site www.deviantinvestor.com.

He is a retired accountant and business manager with over 30 years of experience studying markets, investing, and trading.

Many years ago he did graduate work in physics. He currently lives in Granbury, Texas with his wife.

14261156R00085

Printed in Great Britain
by Amazon.co.uk, Ltd.,
Marston Gate.